Yours, Brett

Also by Gertrude Samuels

FICTION

Of David and Eva

Adam's Daughter

Run, Shelley, Run!

The People Vs. Baby

NONFICTION

B-G: Fighter of Goliaths—
The Story of David Ben-Gurion

The Secret of Gonen:
Portrait of a Kibbutz
in the Six-Day War

PLAYS

The Assignment

The Corrupters

Of Time and Thomas Wolfe

Yours, Brett

Gertrude Samuels

LODESTAR BOOKS
E. P. Dutton   New York

Library of Congress Cataloging-in-Publication Data

Samuels, Gertrude.   Yours, Brett.

Summary: When her father leaves home to marry
another woman and her mother is unable to care for
her, young Brett spends the next ten years in a
variety of foster homes.
    [1. Foster home care—Fiction]   I. Title.
PZ7.S193Yo 1988   [Fic]   87-36658
ISBN 0-525-67255-9

Published in the United States by E. P. Dutton,
2 Park Avenue, New York, N.Y. 10016,
a division of NAL Penguin Inc.

Published simultaneously in Canada by
Fitzhenry & Whiteside Limited, Toronto

Editor: Virginia Buckley   Designer: Alice Lee Groton

Printed in the U.S.A.   W   First Edition
10 9 8 7 6 5 4 3 2 1

for Dorothy and Harry

Author's Note

All the characters and the names of persons
in this book are fictional, and any resemblance
to actual persons, living or dead, is purely
coincidental. None has intentionally been
given the name of a living person.

Research for this documentary novel was
done in major cities and small towns across
America, from New York to California. My
thanks go to the scores of children and young
adults in foster care and group care, and to the
many experts in social work, psychology, civil
rights, and the courts, who so frankly shared
their experiences with me.

G.S.

Part One

When, in disgrace with Fortune
and men's eyes
I all alone beweep my outcast state . . .

William Shakespeare, Sonnet 29

1

The California sky had never seemed more fine and more strange to Brett. On one side, it was rose-tinted with white cottony clouds floating lazily in harmony. But where they drifted toward and touched the mountain tops, the clouds darkened abruptly, threatening the fine day.

Lying prone in the garden of Gram's house, her notebook open and waiting, Brett stared up with mixed feelings at the sky's strange and distracting mood. It reflected her own. All morning, she had been torn between elation and unease, struggling to find the right way, the proper words, to share with her classmates. All morning, the words had eluded her. As valedictorian of the high school graduating class—an immense honor—she wanted to write a speech at once honest, inspiring, poetic. Her mood was fighting that.

But why? She knew she loved her years here with Gram and T.J., as she and everyone called Thomas Jayson, her grandfather. They had been as caring as any parents; she wanted to get some of that feeling into her piece. She loved the school that had nurtured her mind, and the teachers who had helped to redirect her thinking away from the earlier, tormented years. She wanted to share that, too.

But the words wouldn't come. Something was wrong. Something deep within her sounded a warning—an old feeling from the old, bad years.

She rose, staring up at the strange sky. She told herself, You know where to go at times like this.

She shoved her notebook, pen, and book of poetry into her bookbag, crossed the grass to the open garage, and wheeled out her bike.

"Gram?"

"Yes, Brett."

Her grandmother, still splendidly youthful, came out on the patio. She was peeling off her oversize yellow rubber gloves, which meant she had finished her household chores.

"Be back soon."

"Okay."

"I'm having trouble with the speech."

"It'll come, Brett."

"I thought it would be easy, fun."

"You'll make it work."

"It's not fun. Something's gone wrong."

"Don't worry, love. It'll sort itself out."

"I hope so."

She dropped her things in the bike basket and, with a wave of her hand to Gram, took off.

Watching Brett in her floppy striped shirt, denim shorts, and sneakers, Gram recognized a touch of the old tension on her granddaughter's face. How far this graceful, long-legged Brett with her searching blue gray eyes, flowing light brown hair, and easy smiles had come from the desperate, pinched-face, sullen child whom a caseworker had sent to her and T.J. on that lonely cross-country flight just three years ago!

Now, though, Gram had glimpsed the old cynical look on Brett's face, as though unwanted thoughts were back, haunting her, interfering. Well, she was off, Gram suspected, to the secret hiding place where, Brett had once said quite candidly, she could think "without interruption from living things."

Gram and T.J. had never questioned it. They could only guess where it might be.

It was a corner of the lovely, historic cemetery at the far end of town.

Years before, when Brett had arrived in Carson Heights, a city child from New York thrown into a small, rural town of landscaped private homes, gentle streams, magnificent palms and pines, she had felt overwhelmed, out of tune with all the natural beauty. She didn't fit. She wanted out. She didn't trust any of it. Things were bound to change and she'd be thrown out again. It had been that way practically from birth, so why should it be different this time? All she longed to find in this new place was a corner somewhere away from people, especially grown-ups, questioning her, interrupting her, ordering her, hurting her.

In the silence and tranquillity of the cemetery, she felt safe.

T.J. had bought her the bicycle the day of her arrival. "You'll need it to get around this old town and go to school," he had told her matter-of-factly, not aware of the turmoil the gift had aroused in her. As she had stammered her thanks in disbelief, stroking the beautiful chrome and leather thing, she recalled the only other time she'd been on a bike. That was in New York. Mac-the-Knife had given her a ride on the bike he'd "borrowed" from the kid next door.

"No, stole!" the kid's father had yelled to the cops whom he'd phoned. "That whole building next door is full of juvenile delinquents and criminals." And Brett had screamed obscenities at the man for calling the cops, because Mac-the-Knife had been in trouble with the law before. The caseworker had to take them both to court; the judge had allowed her friend Mac to stay in the group home and make restitution, and Brett's grandparents had been notified.

What number was that home—the tenth, the twelfth? Did it matter to anyone?

Brett parked her bike, now adorned with Carson Heights High School and football pennants and a brass plate etched with her own name—Brett Jayson—near the juniper tree. One huge, sturdy limb of the tree had turned away from the parent trunk; it lay on the ground under the leafy overhang, making a fine bench for her: a perfect place for reading or writing her poems, or just for thinking.

Today, feeling tense and vaguely troubled, she wanted to

wander about a bit before starting again on her speech. The young dead here had often helped her, in some curious way, to come to terms with her moods. They held no terrors for her, only a kind of camaraderie, as she read anew the legends on some of the old headstones:

Here rests in calm repose
Our young beloved,
Concetta, 13.

In memory of Manuel,
He will live in our hearts
Forever. . . . Aged 10

On a stone sculpture of an open book:

Thus faded a lovely flower,
Our solace for an hour,
Margaret, 12

Some headstones had half toppled into the sandy earth, the wind and weather making their legends indecipherable. She stood near the graves of young servicemen, small American flags fluttering beside bronze plaques, telling of "our fallen Heroes" of long-ago wars.

She always sought out her favorite:

In memory of Sarah Rose,
She filled our hearts and
She made them happy.
Aged 4 years

Just four years. Part of Brett had died at age four.

That was when the father she'd loved and idolized left her and Mama, and went away to marry someone in another state. Ever since, he had gone completely out of her life. She had been named for him, Brett Jayson. She had never stopped wondering about him.

Nor apparently had Mama. Lovely, feckless Mama, his high school sweetheart whom he'd married when she was eighteen. Mama drank a lot and sought new friends in strange places. She had given young Brett into care—foster home care, group home care—"just for a few weeks, baby, till I get a job." With her mysterious green eyes, streaky blonde hair, and sensual carriage of a dancer, which she once was, Mama said she wanted to model.

She never found the job. She did find other men, and brought them home with her. For a time, Mama seemed to have money enough to keep Brett out of care, but not for long—especially after some men wanted to take Brett into bed with them. Brett would scream and run to hide under her own bed.

The few weeks in care spread into months, and in the early years, Brett couldn't seem to stop crying for Daddy. She never heard from him.

Until she was old enough to understand, she felt she was fighting dragons every day of her life.

Now, Brett stood by her juniper bench, wondering about this strange day. She was dimly aware that just beyond the white picket-fence enclosure, the world was bustling along with interstate trucks and cars and cyclists, their sounds reaching her eerily as though from an echo chamber. She puzzled over what had triggered her decision to come here today. And at last, shrugged it off.

Hey, what's the problem?

I don't see any dragons to kill here.

So, some places I've been are the pits.

Not this place, though.

Not home with Gram and T.J.

Hey, how about "Blessed are the *living!*"

The *caring!*

That's not too shabby. I can use that.

She settled herself on the bench and reached for her notebook. After a moment, she began to write.

Brett took the long way home. She was rather pleased with her rough draft, the poetic quotations she had selected. She ran her bike into the space next to the old Chevy. As she carried her things to her room in the rambling, ranch-style house, she realized that she was famished. She made for the kitchen and the aromas of Gram's cooking, when T.J.'s voice called: "Brett, New York's been trying to reach you!"

"What?"

"Someone in New York has been phoning all afternoon. Says it's urgent. Here."

T.J. handed Brett the message. It was from Brownie, her old caseworker in New York at Second-Chance House, the group home where Brett had once lived. The long-distance operator had given Brownie her number.

Brett's hand was shaking as she took the paper, all that day's strange emotions welling up again.

"Urgent, T.J.?"

The big, rumpled, white-haired man with his quiet ways planted a kiss on top of her head. He said, "Not to worry. Go place the call."

Brett sat on the high stool at the serving bar in the family room, which separated the kitchen from the den. She hesitated picking up the phone.

"Want me to leave, Brett?"

"Oh, no, T.J. But I feel funny."

"Now, don't anticipate. I'll get Gram."

The call was being completed as Gram came.

"Hello, Brownie. This is Brett. You okay?"

The grandparents stood silent during the long pause that followed, aware that Brett's face began to drain of its rosy color. They heard Brett gasp into the telephone, then wail, "Oh, no! It can't be! Oh, Brownie! Oh, damn, damn, *damn!*"

They stood immobilized. T.J.'s arm went around Gram's shoulder in a hard grip. Then Brett was crying, moaning, "Yes, I'll be there. I'm coming! Take care, Brownie!"

She hung up and sat staring at the phone with disbelief.

T.J. said quietly, "Gram, I think we could all do with some hot tea."

They made Brett drink the tea first.

They waited, sharing without knowing why, the girl's horror and pain.

Brett said brokenly, "It's about my friend, Malcolm. It's in the papers back East. He'd been in all those foster homes and juvenile centers, more than me even. Him and his younger brother, Petey."

She gulped some tea.

"Malcolm—he never used that name, said it was his father's and he hated it. He liked to be called Mac-the-Knife. Well, he would never be separated from his brother. That's the one thing the brothers did fight for, to stay together. But Brownie said someone recently adopted Petey. I guess because he's never been in real trouble like Mac. They didn't want Mac; the worker said he'd have to stay in the group home. After Petey went away, Mac got depressed and quit school."

"What's happened, Brett?" asked T.J.

"Oh, T.J.!" she cried. "He'd stolen something, some cassettes from a record shop. He didn't care anymore what he was doing. He thought the cops were going to arrest him. He was afraid he'd be thrown out again, or worse, maybe jail. So yesterday, he got a revolver, Brownie said, and he went to Central Park and he shot himself in the head."

"Oh, good God!" Gram said. She clasped Brett to her, and wept with her.

"He left a note," Brett said. "He wanted to feel I'd come and be at his funeral. Said he doesn't want a sermon. Wants me to say one of my poems. I have to go."

"Of course," said T.J.

"There was a time when Mac and Petey and some other kids were sort of my only lifeline," said Brett.

"I understand."

"I'll help you pack," said Gram.

Oh, strange and terrifying day, she thought on the plane to New York. All the portents had been in place.

The changing sky, both sunny and angry.

Her restlessness.

Her driving need to get to her secret hiding place.

Sarah Rose . . .

Oh, Mac, Mac, why did you have to go crazy?

Or did you finally think that only the world had gone crazy?

Throwing away kids like they're pieces of paper?

Making them outcasts.

Take care, Mac.

Never forget you.

How could I? We were . . . family. For a time.

2

A family? Of hundreds, maybe thousands, of kids over the years. The picture always shifting like a human kaleidoscope, with kids of different ages and ethnic backgrounds—white, black, brown—being thrown together, then torn apart, shifted from one place to another, having no control over their lives or their destiny. No use trying to hook up with new friends, or with new schools; they'd shift and disappear soon enough.

Nothing stayed the same.

You got taken, or you got passed over.

No one asked what the kids wanted or needed.

No one listened to the kids.

No one asked Brett.

As far back as she could remember, Brett wanted it to be the way it once was with Mama and Daddy. That was when Mama was young and pretty and popular. She liked lots of parties and people around her who were with it, cool.

Daddy was the opposite—tall, trim, mild-mannered. He had married Mama just three months before Brett was born. He was a loner who attended a community college and clerked at a supermarket most nights. He resented the party scenes that disrupted his studies. He seemed to find the most happiness at home with Brett, reading her stories and nursery rhymes, waiting for her to put in the last line of each rhyme. She would tease him, holding out on the line sometimes, their private joke. Then he'd hug her or toss her up, and call her "my little witch."

There was a lot of drinking at Mama's parties. The fights over that between her and Daddy got worse, sometimes in front of the others.

"These are my friends!" Mama would yell.

"I need some peace around here, Joyce!"

"An' I need some *life!*"

"Every night?"

"It is not every night!"

"Seems like it."

"Then why don't you get lost?"

The others would start to leave, and Mama would cry out, to cover her embarrassment, "Hey, he's really weird, ain't he? Wait for me!" She'd leave with them.

Daddy would stand like a statue beside Brett in the room, while the stereo was shrilling some rock, the cocktail table littered with bottles, glasses, smoking cigarette butts, and broken crackers.

Brett would stare up at him miserably, the tears starting. He'd say gently, "Help me clean up, Brett."

He would turn off the stereo, and after they'd cleaned the mess away, they'd read together until she fell asleep.

Things went on like that until just after Brett's fourth birthday, with the commotion and fights getting worse. Sometimes, Mama stayed away all night, and Daddy had to leave Brett with neighbors while he went to his classes. At last, Daddy complied with Mama's suggestion: He did "get lost." He transferred to another state and college, let the lawyers call it desertion, and divorced Mama. But after he married someone else, it was as if he had divorced them both.

Mama explained bitterly, "That new wife is really gross. He wrote that a condition of the marriage is he must sever all relations with us—with *us!* They are going to start life together as if we don't exist. How romantic!"

"You mean I can't see Daddy?"

"That's her condition."

"Why?"

"Who knows."

"Forever?"

"Seems like it, Brett."

"It's all your fault!" cried Brett. "I want my Daddy. I don't want him to divorce me."

Mama pulled Brett close to her.

"What can we do, Mama, to get him back?"

"Nothing. He's married to someone else now."

"So?"

"So he has to cut all ties to us."

"Does he have to?"

"Apparently, he *wants* to, baby."

Brett persisted, confused. "Doesn't he want me anymore?"

"Maybe it's not his fault," said Mama unhappily. "He'll do anything for peace. That's his way. Well, she can lay down this sleazy condition, but she forgets one thing."

"What?"

"That we *do* exist. Nothing she can do about that."

Next day, when Brett went to school, she told the kids around her in a tone of curious excitement, "My Mama and Daddy are divorced. I'm divorced. Now I'm like you."

That year, Brett had her first taste of foster care.

Mama was going to modeling school on the little money that Daddy sent her under court order. It meant Brett was often left with neighbors after school; or in the street, dirty and hungry, if neighbors weren't available. One worried neighbor reported the situation to the cop on the beat. That day, he took Brett to the station house, filled out some forms, and phoned in a report to the local branch of Adoption and Foster Care Services. A telex came back that a caseworker was on her way to assess the situation in the home. She herself walked Brett back home, a young, thin woman, tired looking and carrying a bulging briefcase as though, Mama said later, it was full of kids' lives.

Mama complained that it was just some interfering old gossip who had told on her. The caseworker said dryly that perhaps Brett should go into foster care for a few days until Mama could arrange better hours, "so the child can be properly cared for."

Brett clung to Mama. She said no one was going to take

her away from Mama. The worker smiled her patient smile. She said, "The last thing we want—the worst thing—is for a child to come into care and be separated from the parents."

"Of course," Mama said, relieved.

The worker went on evenly, "The second worst thing is if the child is in imminent physical danger, or abused. Then the child can be removed immediately."

"Abused! There's no abuse in my house."

"I'm glad to hear that."

"What are you going to report?"

"A neglect report has already been telexed."

Mama was shaken. "What happens now?"

"For the moment, nothing. I'll come back again to see if you've rearranged your hours so as to look after Brett." She made some notes.

"When?"

"Oh, sometime soon."

She sounded purposely vague.

Mama did try. She was frightened, threatened, by the sudden awful majesty of the law on Brett's behalf. But she seemed unable to sort out her life. She missed her husband and his take-charge ability; she couldn't deal with job seeking or job training; she couldn't cope with responsibilities alone. What she found were new friends in the local bars. She brought one or two of them home, carrying their own bottles, and sometimes they stayed through the night.

The caseworker arrived unannounced one such evening. When she and Mama went to look for Brett, they found her hiding under her bed.

The worker was shocked.

She said, "It's all right, Brett. Come on out."

"Not till he's gone away," said Brett.

Mama yelled, in fear of the worker, "He's going! Come out now, you hear!"

The worker said, "It's only me, Brett. Won't you please come out and say hello?"

Brett came out then. She was sobbing.

"I don't like those people, Mama."

"Shut up! I mean . . . it won't happen again."

The worker said, "I'll stay here with Brett while you say good night to your friend, Mrs. Jayson."

"What do you mean?"

"We have to talk—you and me and Brett."

The caseworker listened silently as Brett blurted out her fear of the man.

"She's exaggerating," said Mama with a nervous laugh.

The worker said, "Look, I'm what's known in our jargon as a 'protective service person.' That mean anything to you?"

"No."

"Well, very simply, for her protection, I think Brett should go into foster care . . ."

"No, I won't allow it!"

". . . to help you as well as the child. Say for a few weeks. She's a scared little girl; surely you see that."

"Oh, baby, I don't want you to go!"

"You have no choice," the worker said toughly, "because that's going to be my recommendation to the court. And you'll be assigned a counselor on your problems."

"What problems you talking about?"

"You're an alcoholic, Mrs. Jayson. You're bringing men home with you who scare Brett. I think you've been abusing this child."

"Abusing her!"

"Brett told it in her own words, with her own actions. I'm taking her with me. We'll get her a temporary placement."

Mama yelled, "You can't do that!"

"Now, be reasonable," the worker said patiently. She had obviously dealt with similar situations a hundred times. "We don't want the cops in, do we? Embarrass you with the, uh, gossips? It may be for only a few weeks. Give you a chance to straighten out."

"What does she mean, Mama?"

Mama was struggling to get a handle on her emotions. "Maybe . . . for a few weeks, darling."

"I don't want to go. I want my Daddy!"

Mama said heavily, "It'll give me time to find some work, baby."

"That's right, Brett," said the worker. "We don't like to separate kids from their parents, you remember?"

She pulled some papers out of her briefcase, ran her forefinger down a list. "Can I use your phone, Mrs. Jayson? It's late, and I need to work fast to find a placement tonight for Brett."

"Can't she stay here tonight?"

The worker didn't hesitate. "No. I won't take this responsibility, after what I've seen. Tomorrow morning at nine o'clock I want you in Family Court, and I'll be there with Brett. The judge can decide what's best for now."

"You mean, he'll decide what *you* recommend!" Mama said spitefully.

"Something like that," the worker said, staying quiet but firm.

She put through a call, and as Mama and Brett listened, she said, "That's right. It's temporary. Yes . . . okay then. No, no trouble at her age." Then a minor explosion from the worker: "For Chrissake, she's only going on five! . . . So, okay. In about an hour."

As expected, the judge, severe and threatening in his black robe on his high bench in Manhattan Family Court, went along with the worker's recommendation. Mama had dressed carefully for the occasion: no makeup, simple dark suit, and pumps. She sat stony-faced when the judge told her, "This arrangement is temporary, you understand? Your daughter will go home to you when we're satisfied you can provide for her decently. Do you have anything to say?"

Mama, terrorized by her surroundings, shook her head.

The judge said, "Speak up, madam, for the record."

Mama said, "No."

No one asked Brett if she had anything to say.

The proceeding took less than five minutes. The judge stamped some papers, arranged for a reappearance in court in four weeks, and tossed the papers aside. A uniformed officer of the court called for the next case.

Mama stumbled out of the courtroom in shock. The worker stood aside while Mama said good-bye to Brett, wiped away her tears, and murmured again and again, "Just for a few weeks, baby."

Then the worker took Brett back to her temporary foster home.

3

Home was a two-bedroom, railroad apartment in the Bronx, rented by Mr. and Mrs. Benton. They were an old-looking couple with a sixteen-year-old son, Martin, and two young girls in care. Brett was assigned to an army cot in the room with eleven-year-old Janet and her sister, fourteen-year-old Cathy. Martin slept on the living room couch.

While the older kids were in school and Mr. Benton went to work on his construction job, the house felt unnaturally quiet, even cozy. Mrs. Benton, who had snow-white short hair and vague, tremulous eyes behind steel-rimmed glasses, seemed to like Brett's company. She let Brett help her make up the beds and do some dusting. She took her to the su-permarket and let Brett choose what she wanted for lunch—hamburger and orange soda. But she didn't enroll her in school. "We don't know if you're staying, do we, child?"

When the others came from school and put on their records and television, or horsed around, the apartment became bedlam. Martin would come into the girls' room, stretch out on Cathy's bed, and smoke, while Cathy laughed and sometimes sat on him.

Brett would run to Mrs. Benton in the kitchen, repeatedly asking, "Can I go home, please?"

"The worker's coming. She'll tell us when."

The worker didn't show up for more than a month. Cathy said contemptuously, "That's all right with the old lady. She's getting more'n $200 a month from the state for each one of us, so that's a great gig for her."

"She's a nice lady," said Brett. "But I want to go home."

Janet, lying on the floor with her homework spread around her, looked up for a moment. She said, not unkindly, "Don't count on it, kid. This here's our—what number, Cathy?—fifth, sixth foster home. They've been shunting us around since I was your age."

"Why? Don't you have a mama?"

Cathy said, "I was kicked out."

"Me, too," said Janet.

"Are you staying here forever?" Brett asked, shocked.

"What's forever?" said Cathy in a joking way. "No one gives a damn about us."

Janet said moodily, "Cathy's gonna get us kicked out again, if she doesn't cool it with Martin."

"You know, Janet, you've got a mouth problem," said Cathy.

"My mama wants me to come home," said Brett.

"Then whyn't she come and get you, hey?"

"She will. You'll see."

Mama didn't come.

"They've been piling cases on me," the caseworker groaned to Mrs. Benton. "I had to keep postponing the court appearances. Brett, how are you doing?"

"She's no trouble at all, miss."

"Can I go home now?"

"Tell you what, Brett. How about if we go visit your mother?"

Mrs. Benton looked alarmed. "Shouldn't her mother come here? I mean, won't it affect what the state signed with me, if Brett doesn't come back?"

"I think Brett misses her mother," the worker began again, Brett hanging eagerly on her words, nodding. "I won't do anything the court hasn't ordered. I can't."

"I'll go get my things," said Brett.

"No, don't do that, dear. Not yet. It's only a visit. Then, we'll see."

It was early evening when they got to Mama's house. They weren't expected, of course, and the apartment was disheveled, littered with a tangle of clothes and bottles. Mama was in a torn housecoat, her eyes bloodshot, her words slurred, as she managed to say, "Look who's here!"

Brett hurled herself at Mama and cried a bit. "You never came! You didn't keep your promise!"

"Oh, baby, I've missed you," said Mama, cuddling her, as she eyed the caseworker.

The worker didn't bother even to sit down. She could smell marijuana as well as beer and liquor. She asked bluntly, "What are you using, Mrs. Jayson?"

"What do you mean?"

"Are you seeing your counselor?"

"Yes. I've got an appointment . . . I think . . . next week." Mama was confused. "No, wait a minute, I'll just show you."

She fished around in her handbag; then she dumped its contents out on the cocktail table, and found an official-looking card with dates on it. She showed it triumphantly to the worker.

"This was set for yesterday," the worker said. "Did you see her yesterday?"

Mama studied the card for a long moment. "So I forgot," she said.

The worker wrote something down. Abruptly, she asked again, "What are you using?"

"Nothing. I swear it."

"You're lying, Mrs. Jayson."

"So maybe a little pot. Just now and then."

"And coke?"

"No, no, no coke. Anyway," said Mama, smiling ingratiatingly, "I haven't got money for coke."

"For crack, maybe?"

"Yeah, it is cheaper—" Mama caught herself. "I mean, I'm not addicted or anything. But I need—something, to relax, you know."

"And you expect me to recommend that Brett come back here?" the worker asked.

"Yeah, I do. She's my daughter."

For a moment, Brett thought the worker might relent.
Mama was holding her tight, smoothing her hair, kissing
her. The worker had stopped writing as she pondered. Then
the moment was shattered.

A large man, unshaven and barefoot, in his shorts, stumbled out of the bathroom.

"Halloo . . . visitors?" He sounded drunk. "And what a
pretty little one!" He lurched forward and tried to pat Brett
on her bottom. Mama pulled her away, muttering, "Go and
get your clothes on, stupid."

"Who you callin' stupid, stupid?"

The worker said, "We'd better go along, Brett."

"He's my friend, is all!" Mama cried. "He's helping me
to get a job."

"Doing what, Mrs. Jayson?"

"Well, he's got—a lot of connections. Tell her, Reggie."

"I think if Brett stays where she is a little longer, until the
court decides—" the worker began.

"Court?" the man burst in. "What court, hey?"

"Come along, Brett," the worker said.

Brett looked at the man.

"Mama, I don't want to go, but—"

The man came close to her again, peering into her face,
and she shrank back.

Mama said heavily, "Yeah, you go with the lady, Brett.
Just for now. I'll come for you, later."

"You promise, Mama?"

"Yeah, I promise. Now don't be worrying, baby."

She kissed Brett, and hurried her and the worker out.
They were seeing too much. In fact, the last things that
Brett and the worker heard were the exchange of shouts:

"You didn't say nothin' about no goddamn court, Joyce. What's it all . . ."

". . . don't involve you. . . ."

". . . an' I don't want to get involved! Do your buys somewhere else, you crazy broad!"

"Cool it, you big ape! It's nothin' to do with you!" And Mama, pleading, "Oh, please, please, Reggie!"

The temporary care at the Bentons' went on for months. Then for a year. Then two years. Mama came a few times, the court having ordered her to make visits. Mrs. Benton enrolled Brett in school. She was fond of her, she told the worker, reporting that Brett often cried herself to sleep, calling for "my daddy."

On her own initiative, the worker decided to write to Brett's father, whom she had traced. She was to tell the judge later, in her summary of Brett's case, that she felt someone had to take a positive step. She was aware that, under the divorce decree, custody had been awarded to the mother. But surely the father, who had remarried and lived with his wife in another state, had rights and should be interested in his daughter's welfare, she said.

She couldn't have been more wrong.

The letter, typed on the stationery of the Adoption and Foster Care Services, addressed to Mr. Brett Jayson in Sioux Falls, South Dakota, telling him that young Brett had been in foster care for over two years and longed to see her father, actually needed him, was returned to her with a note; it was written and signed by the new wife. It said, in short, impersonal sentences, that she and her husband had no responsibility for the child; that the mother had custody; that they didn't want their life interfered with; that as far as they were concerned, they had only one child, their son, Thomas.

The denial of Brett's existence—as daughter, as human being—was clear.

The worker was furious at the callousness of the reply. After she had calmed down, she wrote again, this time requesting an acknowledgment from the father. Her letter was returned unopened. The envelope was marked and underlined: "Not acceptable. Return to sender."

She placed copies of the letters, and the unopened one, in the growing file on Brett Jayson.

Later, in a staff conference with her fellow caseworkers, Brett's worker let go a blast at the man who would reject his daughter.

"How did he get to be such a bastard?" she asked no one in particular.

"Practice," her supervisor said dryly.

"And she's another, that new wife."

"So he's weak or cowardly or both, not to have inquired himself about Brett long before you wrote. And he has a neurotic wife. Is that state of affairs new to us?"

"And Brett becomes another statistic," the worker said wearily, "to add to all the other statistics—the million kids like her in the country, denied or thrown away by their natural parents."

"All we can do," the supervisor said, "is do our job, and not get hooked on these kids."

The worker said, "Do you think I should be taken off this case then?"

"No. You're having ordinary human emotions. Just don't

get carried away by them. What about this mother?"

"She's an addict, and I think she's on the streets. She keeps promising to accept counseling. Never keeps her promises."

"Maybe the time's come to tell her that unless she rehabilitates herself, we'll recommend a severance of her parental rights. Give Brett up for adoption," the supervisor said. "Try that one out on her."

Mama yelled at the worker, "Give Brett up for adoption! Never! You can't do that!"

"The court can, Mrs. Jayson, unless you change."

"Oh, I will. Believe me, I think of Brett all the time. I pray I get her back soon. I have to get her back! I can get a job, straighten out this place, stay clean. I can change, you'll see," Mama said earnestly, believing herself.

4

Life was beginning to take on a dreamlike quality for Brett at age eight.

She felt she didn't belong to anyone, except maybe to Cathy who, by turns, mothered her and bullied her the way she did Janet. Cathy would make them stay out of the bedroom when she wanted to be there alone with Martin. At last, Mrs. Benton, in her passive way, became worried about the two older kids.

She told Mr. Benton, "I don't want Cathy getting pregnant while she's in care here. We're responsible. And she's influencing the other kids—well, she's bad for them."

Mr. Benton said, "She can't teach our Martin anything he don't already know." Tired from his heavy work with the construction gangs, all he wanted when he got home was his dinner, his television sports channel, and early bed. "Hell, those kids are our bread and butter. Don't go lousing it up. But maybe," he said, relenting, "I should speak to Martin."

Cathy was furious when she learned that Mrs. Benton had also expressed her worry to the worker. But her sister was frightened. She said, "Where'll they ship us this time?"

"Can't you go home?" asked Brett.

Cathy said contemptuously, "My mother kicked me out in the first place. We don't get along. I walk into my house and everything I do is wrong." She paused, remembering, then went on in a bitter tone, "She's never satisfied with what I do, what I say. Then she gets mad and tells me to leave. A minute later, after she beats up on me, she regrets it. Right now, she wants us to come back, because she's lonely. I can tell."

Janet said, "I always stick with Cathy."

"Listen, the only reason I go to school is I want that diploma. I want a job, so I'll never have to go back. She never believes anything I tell her, like . . ."

Janet pleaded, "Stop, Cathy, please!"

". . . like the time with my stepfather."

"Not in front of Brett," Janet said, close to tears. "She's just a little kid."

"Not too little to hear it," Cathy retorted. "It happened to me when I was younger than her."

"I always want to throw up when you talk about it," said Janet.

"The worker said I *should* talk about it. It's good for me to get it out. An' maybe it'll protect other kids, to know about it." Cathy hesitated, though.

Brett said, "Tell me, I want to know." She was mystified and curious.

"It's really why I won't go home," Cathy said, after a long pause. "I was five when I started getting abuse from my stepfather. He began coming in my room. I was real little, I didn't know what was going on. He would always tell me, this is the right thing to do. And I would hurt and cry myself to sleep. I would always ask God, Why are you making me go through all this pain? This went on for years."

Janet said, "I didn't know about it then."

"I was so scared," Cathy went on. "I would cry and say I was going to tell my mother. He said if I did, he was going to kill me. Then my grandmother saw what was going on, and she told my mother. But my mother wouldn't believe it. She promised she was going to leave him, and I thought, Oh, good, it's going to end. Then she'd say, 'No, this isn't happening,' and 'Why are you stupid enough to let it go on?' I was about nine, ten years old. He . . . he really messed me up. He messed me up good. But the worst thing was, she was blaming me, shouting at me, 'Why did you let him do this?' She wouldn't believe the truth!

"So that's how all our quarrels began, and I swore it wouldn't happen to my sister. He wasn't going to do it to her."

Janet cried, "You have to stop thinking about it!"

"I can't. My mother never left him. Instead, she kicked me out. I took Janet with me. He's gone now. He knows I talked about it to my worker. I guess he got scared and disappeared. But I can't forgive my mother. To this day, she won't believe it was happening all those years."

Brett said, not understanding all of it, "But now, is it different for you—I mean, with Martin?"

Cathy said harshly, "Well, of course! He's my boyfriend, and we like each other."

Janet said, "You're gonna get us kicked out."

"Oh, yeah? Soon I'm going to be old enough," said Cathy in a hard voice, "so no one can kick me out of anywhere!"

Mrs. Benton called the worker in.

"My son's to blame as much as Cathy," she said. "I don't know how to handle him anymore. Perhaps I should take in only boys. Do you think you can transfer the girls? Make it easier on them—and on me."

It took the worker several weeks. The city and private agencies in New York State were overwhelmed with tens of thousands of such cases to place—many of them kids like Cathy who had been kicked out of their homes, or had run away from bad family situations.

Cathy and Janet were transferred to a diagnostic center until a new home could be found for both of them together. Brett was placed in another temporary foster home, this time in Brooklyn. It meant a new set of parents, new school, the loss of friends, also the loss of her worker. A new caseworker was assigned to her.

She felt abandoned, twisted up inside, panicky. She cried a lot, sometimes all night.

In class, she often struggled to stay awake. She would stare around the room with hostility at the others, who seemed happy, secure—boisterous kids living at home. Normal. One question kept popping into her head: Why is this happening to me?

At recess, she would shun the other kids, preferring to stay in study hall and read. She was drawn to the poetry books, and wrote her own poems.

She hated the crowded conditions at home. Now, she shared a bed with her foster parents' baby, who sometimes wet the bed.

When Mama came once on a visit, bringing a pretty new sweater and a bag of cookies, Brett threw them back at her. "I hate it here!" she cried. "Why can't I go home? Why can't I go to Daddy if you don't want me?"

Then she was hugging and holding Mama. Mama would soothe her, and promise to take her home as soon as her counselor said she was strong enough. Daddy wasn't sending enough money, and she was on welfare and food stamps.

"Things are gonna change, you'll see," she told Brett earnestly. "I have this friend . . ."

She put the sweater on Brett, and hugged her. They sat close to each other, sharing the cookies.

Then Mama would disappear for another three or four months.

5

By the time Brett was eleven, she had been transferred from foster home to foster home, six in all, often for rebelliousness. In despair with her now-fragile life-style, she resisted authority, was turning more inward. She had grown tall and thin; her light brown hair fell carelessly over half her face most of the time, as though veiling her feelings and secret thoughts. Her best feature, the wide-set blue gray eyes, stared back hard at people, skeptical, often insolent. She did the minimum of what was expected of her, not caring, she told herself bitterly, since she believed that nothing would last anyway.

The foster homes she experienced did little to help her self-esteem. In one of them, the mother, Mrs. Bullitt, was a huge woman of three hundred pounds who demanded that after school Brett do the general cleaning up and laundry. There were four kids in care, and Brett was also expected to bathe and feed the two infants and baby-sit while Bullitt indulged her own addiction—bingo at the neighborhood church.

When at last Brett stormed to her room, refusing to do the chores any longer—"I've got my homework . . . have to go to the library"—the big woman caught her by the hair, and swung her around.

She shouted, "Little slut, you'll do as I tell you or I'll lock you in the closet with the vacuum."

"I'm not your slave!" Brett shouted back, as she raced out of the house. She phoned her worker.

"Am I supposed to be abused in this place?" she demanded.

"Of course not," replied the startled worker. "What's been happening?"

"This Bullitt shouldn't be in charge of kids," Brett said. "I'm not going back there. I'll . . . I'll run away."

"Take it easy, Brett," the worker said. "Now, wait outside the house for me. I'll get there within the hour. Promise?"

Brett promised. Anyway, she had personal things inside that she wasn't about to give up.

That night, the worker took Brett and her small suitcase to her downtown office—"until I can get the full story straight." Placement elsewhere wasn't possible on such short notice. Brett spent the night sleeping on her worker's desk.

More temporary places followed—a week here, a month

or two there. She thought of Cathy and Janet, sisters, and felt bitterly alone, rejected, kicked out, she reported, "because I wouldn't let myself get hit."

In fact, she was now hitting back. She found herself in foster homes with white and black girls and Hispanics, and the kids all seemed to be fighting with one another. She yearned for privacy. There was none. With her quick temper, she was drawn into pushing and elbowing bouts over imagined or real slurs and thefts: Someone had stolen one girl's soap or another's socks or costume jewelry—or, the very worst, someone's money.

At the counseling sessions, which she was required to attend twice a month, she told her worker, "I'm fighting all the time. I don't know why."

"What do you think you can do about it?"

"I feel like running away."

"Where to?"

"I don't know."

"There are thousands of kids on the streets, runaways, homeless, sleeping in the park, in ditches. You want to join that army, Brett?"

She shuddered. "No."

She never asked to go home now. The worker told her that Mama was too sick, a drug addict who loved her but couldn't take care of her properly. When Brett thought of Mama now, it was always of "poor Mama."

"But what's the good of shuffling me around all these places?" she cried. "How can I stay in school and keep up with my studies?"

The worker said, "I'm going to recommend a different

kind of placement for you: upstate, in a general institution and not a foster home. . . ."

Brett was frightened. "Like in a prison?"

The worker laughed. "No, child, of course not. And it's only temporary. Let's see how you like it, and how they like you. There's a school right there, on campus."

Brett hated it.

In contrast to the private foster homes, the institution was huge, with common dormitories for some fifty girls, up to age seventeen. Discipline was strict, with religious classes and a curfew and, certainly, no fighting allowed.

Brett found herself more isolated and depressed than ever. She felt overwhelmed by the older girls, who mostly ignored the little kids. For all its size, there was curiously no privacy either, except when she could slip into a corner of the small library. Often, she shoved the books and home-work aside, put down her head, and just wept.

Brett's new worker, observing her misery in the library one day, took her for a walk. The spacious lawns were finely manicured, with blossoming borders cared for by the girls. The late spring afternoon held a cold snap, and the sun rode palely high above them as they made for a bench far from the others. Brett tightened her windbreaker against the cold and against her fears.

"What's wrong, Brett?"

She burst out at once, "Oh, please, miss, send me back to the city! I feel so . . . so lost here."

"What else, Brett?"

"What else? I don't know. I'm being punished for something, I guess, and I must deserve it, but this place—it's frightening, it's the pits! I'm sorry, miss . . ." She stumbled, trying to focus her feelings, and cried impulsively, "I just want to find my daddy."

"All right," the worker said briskly. "How about if we write to him?"

"You mean me?"

"Who else? Do you have his address?"

"It's in my file. But the letters always come back."

"Oh? Well, why not write one of your own? Very personal. Tell him how much you miss him, and want to visit him after all these years. How about sending him a poem?"

Brett was excited. The worker knew about her poems. "You think I should?"

"Do you have a favorite poem?"

"Yes, I do. I was thinking of Daddy when I wrote it. Want to see it?"

Brett brought it out of her notebook.

The social worker read it out loud. She stared at Brett for a long moment, her eyes misting over.

"I think he'll love this," she said. "Copy it into your letter to him."

In her most careful handwriting, Brett wrote:

Dear Daddy,
    I hope you're well and happy. I miss you and love you very much. Since you left us, I have had to live in many kinds of places because Mama isn't feeling too good. Now I'm twelve years old, in this big place, far from New York, but I hope to be able to

leave it soon. I hear that I have a young
brother now, Tommy. That's nice.

I would like to visit you very much. I love
poetry, which you taught me to do. So I'm
copying below my favorite poem to share with
you. I call it "My Dream."

My Dream

There's a dream in my head
It has its ups and downs,
But mostly it's a wishing bird,
Singing away the frowns.

The dream makes me hopeful,
I try to hold it fast
So I take it to a lovely land,
To settle in at last.

When can I come and visit you, and meet my
brother? Are you in a lovely land? Please
answer soon. I really miss you, Daddy.

> With love and kisses,
> Yours, Brett

She showed the letter to her worker, who said it was
something she could be proud of. In fact, she copied it into
Brett's file, posting the original by registered mail, return
receipt requested, to assure Brett of its arrival and proper
signature.

It was received all right. Brett got the receipt back from
Sioux Falls, South Dakota. But it was signed *Mrs. B. Jayson.*

She never got an answer.

6

Later, when Brett could look back calmly on her life, she would date her changed feelings toward her father and his new wife from the moment of the return receipt, and the denial of a reply.

For from that time, she began to stop yearning and crying for Daddy. She managed to say some of this out loud, at last, at the peer meetings. The dorm to which she had been assigned had group sessions with a counselor periodically, "to ventilate your feelings, get things off your chest, stop punishing yourselves," as the Fact Sheet handed to each resident proclaimed.

"We are," the Fact Sheet added, "a crisis intervention center for runaway, homeless, and abused young people. This is a short-term residential center. Group counseling is offered, and family members, especially parents, are urged to attend these meetings."

Mama never showed up. The social worker also noted in Brett's file her father's rejection. In fact, the worker added in a cynical footnote: "Brett now appears to be another human throwaway." That note would also, she felt, cover her responsibility, should the question ever arise in court as to whether all that could be done for Brett had been done.

At the peer session, with the kids seated in a semicircle, the counselor threw out a question or two to move the meeting along. Brett listened closely when Melody spoke. She was a pretty sixteen-year-old, curly haired Hispanic with a nervous tic in one cheek, eager to be heard first.

She said, "I was always beating up on kids."

"Tell us why, Melody."

" 'Cause when they hit me, I'd want to hit them back harder, right?"

"Are you angry?"

"Yeah, I used to be. Real angry."

"You haven't beaten up on anyone here, have you?"

"I ain't been here long." The others laughed.

"Was there anyone in those other places you could talk to?"

"Nah."

"How many places, Melody?"

"Thirty-eight. This is my thirty-ninth."

"Oh, come on, Melody . . ."

"I swear to God! It's in my records, ma'am."

"How long did you stay in those places?"

"Sometimes a day, sometimes a week, or a month. When

we'd fight, my social worker—she'd pull me out. She'd put me somewhere else."

"What was your anger about? Have you thought about that, Melody?"

"Yeah, I have. It's, well, my mother. I don't hate her, she's a mother, right?" Her voice hardened. "But I don't love her, and I don't call her Mom anymore. I call her by her name. I call her Christine . . . her name. She ain't my mother."

The semicircle was quiet, as though mesmerized by Melody's outpouring. How many were identifying with her, Brett wondered, as she heard some tearful sniffs.

"What do you mean, Melody?"

"I don't consider her my mother. She threw me out when I was a child. She didn't bring me up."

"What went wrong?"

"She's sick, I guess. Drinking all the time, and doing drugs. Yeah, she does that, I know."

"And your father?"

"I never met him. Christine said he's a cop. They got a divorce right after my sister was born. I was about two years old. I never met him."

"Do you want to?"

"What?"

Brett leaned forward, listening hard.

"Meet him? Get to know him?"

"Nah. I don't want to. Why should I? Why meet him now, after fourteen years?" she cried explosively.

"You have no curiosity about him?"

"Nah. Except, my mother . . . I mean, Christine, she said I look like him. He's a very cute man."

The others burst into laughter again, Melody joining in, like a cathartic for all of them.

"I don't want to split from here, ma'am."

"Why not, Melody?"

"I guess, I could say . . . I'm tired. I don't want to make these places number forty, number forty-one. . . ."

Karen said, "Tired? You can say that about all of us." She was a wisp of a girl, about Melody's age but looking far younger with her thin, drawn face and short-cropped fair hair. "But I figure," she went on, "a lot of what's happening to us is our own fault."

There were shouts from the others:

"It ain't mine!"

"That's dumb talk!"

"What about wasting the little kids?"

"What'd they do?"

"You're just dumping on us!"

Karen insisted, "Well, that's how I feel." Two red spots colored her pale cheeks. "I've been messing up since I was thirteen. I had a liquor problem, hanging out, staying out late, ditching classes. Started experimenting with drugs, pot at first; then acid, coke, mushrooms—you name it. The arguments at home got worse and worse. We had like a wall between me and my mom. And I wasn't willing to do anything 'round the house. Yeah, I'm tired of it, too. This is my eighth place."

"Where was your first placement, Karen?" the worker asked.

"The lockup. For possession."

"Of what?"

"Like I said. Pot, some coke."

"Where did you get the stuff?"

Karen said, "From my mom. She was using."

"What?"

There was a burst of nervous laughter from the others. "Your mother gave you the stuff?"

"Yeah, she turned me on. After that, I got arrested after school, hanging out with a couple of guys. When the cops came, everyone ran, but like a dope, I stood frozen."

More knowledgeable laughter from the others.

"You went to jail?"

"Yeah, juvenile, for a month, till they put me in a foster home, away from my mother. I remember what that judge said to me: 'If you're old enough to do the crime, you're old enough to do the time.'"

"Yuck! He must have said that to a thousand kids," someone said.

"I went home for a while. But I got kicked out by my stepfather when I was fourteen. Always getting into arguments. I had nowhere to go. I started sleeping in the streets, once in a ditch. It was real cold. I was scared. I had to eat ketchup, I had nothin' else to eat." Her voice was harsh, remembering.

A terrible quiet fell on the small gathering. A knot of fear twisted Brett's stomach, and her head ached. "I wanted to go home pretty bad," Karen was saying. "But they didn't want me back."

The worker asked, "How do you feel now, deep down?"

Karen weighed that for a long moment. "I figure I screwed up. I figure it's time I did better for myself."

"You telling us it's all been your fault?" someone jeered.

"A lot of it has been. Now, I want to learn how to take one day at a time."

After Karen, for the next hour, others began to spill out their problems and their guts. Most of the talk was downbeat, some of it bitter and rancorous, as they reached for some understanding of their plight. The counselor understood.

She said quietly, "Just off the cuff, the more I listen to you kids, the more I try to fathom where you get the strength, the sheer strength, to go on. You kids are trying to find it. And I'm proud of you."

There was some nodding of heads, and some sheepish grins. They knew that after they spilled it all out, the counselor was "picking them up again."

At last, Brett felt she could speak up.

"I'm leaving here soon, my worker says. I don't know where I'm going again. And the way I feel," she said, choosing her words, "I don't care. I really don't care. I do know one thing: I'm sorry for my mother. She's weak and sick, and I'd like to go home, but I'm scared of that place now with all the things that go on there." She paused. When she began again, her words were measured. "I do have a father. I'm even named for him—Brett. But he doesn't want me. I think there's nothing worse in life than not being wanted. Now, I've stopped wanting him. And I think I hate him. I know now I'll just have to get along without him. All my life."

7

After Charlotte Jayson signed the return receipt for Brett's letter—her husband was at work—she did not hesitate.

She ripped open the envelope, read the letter and poem, promptly tore them into small pieces, and poked them deep into the rubbish of her garbage pail.

Tommy, chewing on some breakfast toast spread with jam that had smeared his upper lip, witnessed the scene thoughtfully. He shoved his round, tinted glasses more firmly up his nose, and brushed some crumbs off his chin.

"Who was it from, Mommy?" he asked.

She wheeled about, startled by her son's presence. "What?"

"Didn't you like the letter?"

Her voice rose. "What are you doing in here with that messy toast? Go wipe your mouth."

She hurried the boy to the kitchen and watched him gulp down the rest of his milk before he grabbed his schoolbag, kissed her, and raced out of the house.

Charlotte wished Tommy hadn't seen her fury with the letter. He was a cheery, bookish boy—"chip off the old block," his father liked to say—with a quick, inquiring mind. She was sure his curiosity about the letter wouldn't end there. But the letter, with its pleading and poetry, had enraged her. The girl was like a thief, she told herself, trying to break the order of Charlotte's world. Wasn't she only protecting her husband against the folly of his first marriage, protecting their son, now eight, against any division of loyalties?

After all, that had been the prime condition she had laid down for their marriage—to forget that there had been anyone in his life before her. The only time she was forced to moderate that vision of perfect commitment was when her husband had demurred at her wish to name their son Brett, after him.

"There is a child already with my name," he said.

"No more! She doesn't exist! You promised!"

"Nevertheless, she has my name."

"But that's all finished with!"

He persisted. "The name is a given. Besides, my parents would object."

At that, she gave in. Reluctantly.

She had never met his parents (her own were long dead), and she had no wish to turn them against her. They were retired ranchers in a small California town, and one day she might need their support: She had ambitions to move her family from Sioux Falls, where she had been brought up by a spinster aunt, to "California Dreamin'," the goal of her favorite song. She was always singing or humming it, and had taught it to Tommy. He was named for T.J., his grandfather.

Charlotte Jayson, with her stubborn ways, was a paradox. Loving, kind, and considerate one minute, she was a harridan and schemer the next. She had known what it was like to be loved and desired only when she met Brett Jayson in the engineering firm where she worked as executive secretary to his boss. When they married, she made him and Tommy the whole focus and fabric of her life, and no one was going to unravel it.

In contrast to young Brett's weak and once lovely Mama, the new Mrs. Jayson was a tall, angular, heavy-breasted woman whose cordial smiles could suddenly shift to tight-lipped anger and whose voice went shrill when she was crossed.

Brett Sr., lonely and at loose ends following his divorce from Joyce and transfer to the Middle West, was only too glad of the sympathy of Charlotte—"a sort of earth mother," he wrote his parents. To be sure, she had peculiar ideas about commitment to a close-knit family that ruled out former relationships. "She can't bear to think I've loved any woman before her," he wrote. But, he said, that would undoubtedly change with their marriage.

It hadn't. If anything, Charlotte demonstrated that she was more than ever jealous of his former life in New York, and uncompromising about cutting dead his former wife and daughter.

For example, when he suggested that he'd like to have his daughter at their wedding, she shot that idea down at once. "There is no daughter and no Joyce in our new life," she told him. Despite some twinges of guilt, he gave in, for the sake of peace, the sustaining faith, he told himself.

His parents wrote that they were troubled about Charlotte's attitude. Early in the marriage, Gram urged him to consider taking in young Brett, "since Joyce isn't able to cope." Gram wrote she'd had reports from caseworkers that the child was neglected, with no real home, and she was yearning for her father.

"I was tempted," he told Charlotte.

"No way! Get that Satan behind thee," she had retorted stridently.

At first, his parents had distanced themselves from the matter, not wanting, they wrote, to interfere. Later, they tried again.

They phoned Charlotte, saying they would fly to Sioux Falls to discuss young Brett with the whole family. But Charlotte said flatly not to bother; she was sure they'd be meeting soon—but in California. She was so unbending that they decided not to stir those muddy waters.

Still, they didn't give up. They got in touch with foster care officials in New York, who promised to locate Brett and have her phone them.

When finally the call came from Brett, it was a disappointment. In a polite but firm voice, Brett declined the eager proposal from Gram to "come to us, darling. For a visit first, if you like. See if you want to make your home with us."

"I can't do that," Brett told her. "I must stay here, near

my mama. She needs me. She's sick. But thank you very much."

"We love you," Gram told her. "Just remember, we're standing by. We want to help."

"How was school, Tommy?"

"Okay, Dad. Except gym. I cut and went to the library."

"I've told you to stop that," said Charlotte. "Talk to him, Brett, you hear! He needs the exercise."

Brett asked, "Do you do it often, Tommy? Cut?"

"Nope. But the gym teacher won't let me play basketball because I wear glasses."

"Did you tell him we shoot baskets in our yard?"

"Sure. He doesn't care. He says I'm too short, anyway, and he wants to train winners."

Charlotte said, "I'll just have a talk with that teacher."

"No, Mommy, you'll only make things worse."

"I'll do it if I want to!"

Brett said quietly, "You'll embarrass him."

"And the other kids will be on my back," said Tommy.

"What d'ya mean?" asked Charlotte.

"Oh, you know . . . mama's boy or something."

"I only know I don't want you cutting class," she said. "Bodybuilding is as important as books."

Brett said, "No more cutting, Tommy, okay?"

"Yeah, but it's boring."

"Boring? That reminds me of a favorite story my dad liked to tell me when I was bored," Brett said. "About meeting a bore while he was out strolling, and the man asked him, 'Hi, there, tell me, what's going on?' 'I am,' my dad said, as he kept going on."

They laughed, and Brett was thankful he had broken the tension.

"Mommy got a letter today she didn't like," said Tommy.

"It was nothing," said Charlotte, her mood shifting again.

"You had to sign for it."

"Just finish your supper, and get to your homework," she said sharply.

Brett asked, "Something important?"

"Nothing of the sort. I threw it out."

"Oh?"

Charlotte cleared her throat. "Just some advertising, about popular diets. I'd sent away for the stuff. You know how I'm keen on health foods."

"So why throw it out?"

Charlotte busied herself scraping food from the supper dishes, carrying them to the kitchen. "'Cause there was nothing new in it. Tommy, I said you've got homework."

Tommy helped himself to three chocolate-chip cookies, excused himself, and went to his room.

Brett said mildly, "You've tried so many fad diets, Charlotte. Why bother to send for more?" Then, seeing his wife's frown, he added in a joking tone, "Do I have to remind you I happen to love the fully developed, mature woman?"

"That what I am? Not like that trash you were married to?"

"Oh, for God's sake, Charlotte!"

"I've seen pictures. She was flat as a pancake."

He said dryly, "Not really. But why be jealous of her?"

"What? Jealous of that . . . that weirdo?"

He left the table then, picked up the evening paper, and

51

tried to settle down in the club chair, hoping the threatening squall would fade. Still, he couldn't resist one impulse. "That letter?" he asked. "Was it really only advertising?"

"That's what I told you, didn't I? Don't you trust me?" Her tone was shrill, defensive.

He turned back to his paper. Silent. At moments like this, he felt trampled on by her.

8

Brett had said at the group session that she didn't care where she was sent from the institution. In fact, she cared deeply about wanting to be near Mama, about wanting some school permanency for a change. Her worker understood—and found Brett a placement with a Manhattan foster family in Greenwich Village.

To be sure, the family was already crowded, with two New York and two Vietnamese girls in an apartment near Washington Square Park. The Asian girls, in their early teens, were strangely quiet—refugees from the boat people who had fled Vietnam. Hong-Lan and Kim-Yen told a horrendous story of having been attacked at sea by pirates. They had hidden themselves while a dozen fellow refugees were robbed, then thrown overboard and drowned by the pirates, who escaped in their powerboat.

Brett was drawn to the shy, thin girls who had survived and now were struggling to learn English and understand the foreign culture.

She liked her new foster parents, retired folk who simply asked to be called Mister and Missus. They occupied one bedroom, while the girls squeezed into the other, with its five army cots, footlockers, and small desk. But the living room was spacious and inviting, with a vaulted ceiling, couches near the fireplace, a television, and a well-polished upright piano. Hong-Lan and Kim-Yen loved the piano—"like ours at home"—and practiced on it daily.

"We promised our parents," they told Brett, "we'd study hard, and not forget them." Their parents had to be left behind in Vietnam. "Fortunately for them," said Missus, "considering what happened on that boat."

The other girls were trouble, according to Missus. They scared Brett with their street smarts, but they also fascinated her with their adventures. Michelle, sixteen, and Josie, fifteen, had belonged to a gang called The Dragons, they told her, and had been court cases for years.

"You're lucky to be cared for here and going to school," Missus warned them, shaking her gray head with worry when she found out they were spending more time in Washington Square Park than in school. The park was a haven for young mothers with infants, but also a magnet for junkies and drug dealers. Open sales were common day or night in the park that was traversed by New York University students on their way to classes. Missus knew the dangerous area well. "You know, any more trouble could put you away for years."

Mister put in, "It would hurt our reputation, too. We're known as very good foster parents."

"Oh, that you are," said Michelle blithely, "best we've ever had." She winked at Josie, and Missus had to wonder what mischief the girls would get into next.

Mama came once, with an apple pie and a bag of fruit, and a small teddy bear for Brett. Mama looked bad, her hair dyed a brassy yellow, the lovely eyes heavily made up, her corduroy pants and sneakers scruffy. Brett held Mama tight, and said in reply to her questions, "It's okay here. When am I coming home?"

Mama replied vaguely, "Soon, baby. Soon as I can save some money."

Brett cuddled the teddy. "I love it, Mama."

Mama said, "It's from my boyfriend. Why don't you write and thank him, Brett?"

Brett stared hard at Mama then. After her mother left, she stuck the brown bear with its glittery button eyes and pretty red ribbon at the bottom of her footlocker and never took him out.

For nearly two years, Brett remained with her new foster parents. She was in the same junior high school as the Vietnamese sisters, who not only quickly mastered English but also stood at the top of their class in math and music.

Missus and Mister were proud of those charges. They told Brett the girls were real achievers and models for the others. Brett would agree silently; her own grades were poor, next to failing. The only modest interest she showed was in the reading and writing classes. More and more, she was given to passionate outbursts if criticized. When her pain and frustrations overwhelmed her, she would even scream at the girls during piano practice, "Stop it! You're driving me crazy! You don't own this house!"

They would stop and gaze at her so sadly that she couldn't stand their patient, forgiving looks and would grab up her books and race out to the park. She had a favorite bench near the great arch, away from the infants' playground. There she made herself concentrate on homework. She forced herself to block out thoughts of Mama, who rarely came now, and who couldn't cope with the real world.

Brett was nearly fourteen, grown shapely and small-waisted, with rounded breasts and graceful legs. She wore her long, stringy brown hair in plaits down her back. Her searching blue gray eyes told their own story: Too often they gazed cynically on a world she despised. Other kids, stinging her senses with their joyous noises and laughter, had mothers and fathers. Where were hers? Why was she rejected, unloved?

"Why me?" she would rage inwardly.

Her angers were twisting her away even from those who would be her friends, like Hong-Lan and Kim-Yen, who might have helped. She was sullen with her worker for not coming more often. "I need someone to talk to!"

The worker explained, "Caseloads are too heavy these days—eighty-five kids to look after; papers to prepare; then the court hearings. And," she warned, apprehensive over reports of Brett's problems at school, "we have fewer places for children. Too many kids in trouble are winding up in juvenile detention—and in jail."

"So I'm lucky to be here?" Brett asked sourly.

The worker said, "What do you think?"

She began to truant, accompanying Michelle and Josie on some of their jaunts. She was fascinated by the older girls, who used lots of makeup and heavy metal jewelry and belts; they smoked and had boyfriends in the park. She learned early on that they were using pot and maybe hard stuff, though she knew enough to say no. More than once, when a patrol car drove near them, she was scared and ran home.

One day in school, she gave her angry, hostile mood full rein. The teacher of English composition, Mr. Taylor, a balding, mild-mannered man, told the class to improvise. He wrote the topic on the blackboard: "Things in Life That I Love."

He emphasized, smiling, "Trust yourselves to be forthcoming and honest about your feelings. Be as free as you like."

Brett headed her paper: "Things in Life That I Hate."

First she listed "all the people in this school who should be fired." Curiously, the last named on her list was her father. She printed his name in large letters, BRETT JAYSON, FATHER, and added "because his shadow follows me around the school and life."

Impulsively, she wrote on, taking her teacher's words literally, to be free as she liked:

Who is it shadowing me?
He wears such cunning masks,
He uses them to cover up
His many, moody selves. . . .

Once there was the caring
Mask . . . call it "husband,"
Next the mask we two loved,
That we knew as "Daddy."

Came the time he donned the
Awful mask . . . call it "divorce."
Then slipped behind a newer one,
A fearful one . . . and cruel.

One sees now his moody shift,
It's a frightful mask that says,
"Forget! Forget you were born!
Forget, forget, forget me!"

But here's a mask that is
Not his, that makes a plain reply,
That says, "No, damn you, no! no!
I won't forget! I won't forgive!"

Mr. Taylor called a halt to the writing. He asked monitors
to collect the papers. He scanned them while the murmur-
ous students glanced around, some with confidence, others
with nervous smiles. Brett sat stiffly in her seat, staring into
space. She had poured out the sudden poem in such anger
that a headache began to pinch her temples. She raised her
hand to be excused. But Mr. Taylor shook his head, looking
at her in a puzzled but pleased way.

"Stay a moment, Brett."

"I have a headache, sir."

"Well, no wonder. Uh, I mean, I've just read your paper. Your poem."

The class began to titter. Brett winced.

"A little joke on the school, eh?" said Mr. Taylor. "I'm glad I'm not on your list of villains." The class giggled, some turning to look at Brett curiously. "But overlooking your, uh, jest," he said, clearing his throat, "I'd like to read your poem to the class."

"Oh, no . . . please!" Brett cried.

He hesitated, reacting to her plea. Then he said, "First, because it's clear you composed it off-the-cuff," he went on mildly, "and that takes talent; and second, because the sentiments in it are, I think, universal. Now, Brett, with your permission?"

Universal! There were others, maybe, in this room!

She nodded agreement.

She heard him recite her improvisation slowly and respectfully, projecting each line, making the right pauses, giving her thoughts full value.

Brett was deeply shaken. No one had ever read one of her poems out loud, and to an audience.

There was absolute quiet in the room as he read, and, at the end, a sort of stunned silence. Then a smattering of applause.

Mr. Taylor said, "I'd like to submit it to the school paper."

"Oh, no, not that!"

"Very well. But would you copy it out for me to keep? One day, I hope to publish a book of some of my students' best essays and poems."

Her poem, her angry, universal poem, to be published in a book! There were friendly smiles all around her now. Through a mist of tears, she heard some comments:

"It's so honest, Brett."

"So mysterious . . ."

"I know that feeling, too . . ."

And Mr. Taylor's voice rising above the others: "Go on writing, Brett. Be proud of your talent. What will you call your poem?"

" 'Masks,' " said Brett.

9

Brett had intended her poem to hurt others as she felt hurt. Even to recklessly invite trouble, and get punished for compelling attention to herself, to her needs. Instead, here was Mr. Taylor not only not punishing her but praising her for her originality.

His generosity—for that was what she recognized in her bones—was an immense booster shot to her morale. She had tingled with pride and happiness when he said, in front of the class, "Go on writing. Be proud of your talent."

She would never in her life forget that.

He believed in her.

I have something to be proud of, Mama.

It's mine—no one can take this from me.

I'll write every day.

Everyone in the house was in high spirits with Brett's achievement. Michelle said, "Hey, we have to celebrate." And for once, Missus didn't object when the older girls said they would take Brett out for a treat that evening and be back around eleven.

On the way, Brett asked, "Where to, Michelle?"

"A great place."

Josie said, "See, we're dating these two guys."

Michelle said roughly, "Shut up! It's a surprise."

"But she may not like it."

"So? She's got two legs. She knows how to split."

Brett said, "No problem." She felt very grown-up.

They headed into Washington Square Park. In the early evening, the trees cast long shadows on the paths still shafted by sunlight. The park was crowded and noisy, with people hurrying home from work; students reading or eating snacks on their way to classes—many of them worked during the day; cyclists and skateboard acrobats speeding past one another. And in the midst of the clatter, the human parade of the homeless: some bag ladies taking over benches with their miserable belongings; derelict men sneaking drinks from pint bottles in their jackets; young drifters mooching cigarettes and "any change, ma'am," from passersby or, furtively, trying to make a sale, though the police detail in the park was very heavy.

Brett normally avoided the park at this hour, feeling not a little scared when some lout would whistle after her:

"Hi, beautiful, want some action?"

"Hi, what's the hurry?"

Michelle and Josie clearly had no such fears. In fact, they

seemed to recognize quite a few people, pausing to have a giggle, as they described it to Brett. Then they sauntered on to two waiting figures near the great arch.

"You're late, as usual," the taller of the two greeted them sharply. He was a rugged young man with shiny blond hair, wearing a black leather jacket, a thick gold neck chain, and one earring. He pulled Michelle to him in a tight embrace, at the same time asking suspiciously, "Who's the chick?"

Michelle said, "She lives with us at the home, Nick."

"She's gonna celebrate with us," said Josie. "Say hello to Nick and Leo, Brett."

Josie slid beside Leo, a short, thin young man with heavy-lidded eyes, a developing mustache, and a long black pony-tail. He, too, sported a black leather jacket and one earring, and, as he threw his arm around Josie and pulled her over, he asked, "What's she using?"

Brett stammered, "Using?"

"Don't worry," Michelle said lightly. "That's Leo's hairy way of saying hello."

"Yeah, okay," said Nick, "let's move outta here."

"What's the celebration?" asked Leo.

Michelle told him, and Nick gave a whoop.

"Hey, whaddya know, a poet," said Nick. "And gonna be published."

Brett protested, "That's only a maybe."

"Good enough to get high on," said Leo.

Michelle put in quickly, "Where's this party you promised, Nick? You said someplace special tonight."

"Yeah, I must have ESP or somethin'," said Nick, very pleased with himself. "It's at the NYU Student Center, for starters. Ain't that a coincidence—just the place for uh, intellectuals?" He stumbled over the word.

Josie drew back. "We can't go there. We ain't got ID's. We'll get in trouble."

Nick said with a grin, "You forgettin' I've got connections? They're meeting us near the center, taking us in as their guests. Surprise!"

The girls laughed with delight.

Brett was thrilled to be actually going into the university. Its buildings edged the park; and she'd heard that the Student Center held an art gallery, a theater, radio studios, and a rooftop garden with grand vistas of the park.

Not far from the center, they met three students—two young men wearing blazers and dark glasses, and a young, fair-haired woman dressed all in white, from her silk polo shirt and tailored slacks to her patent-leather pumps. Her dark aviator glasses covered half of her face.

No words of greeting were exchanged. Michelle and Josie pulled Brett to one side, while some sort of ritual was taking place between the others. Brett saw Nick and Leo withdraw tiny vials in plastic from their jackets; then money changed hands. Fast. It happened in seconds.

One student said nervously, "Okay, come on then," and they went to the center. Once inside and past the security guard at the entrance, the three students disappeared.

Nick led his group not to the elevator that would have taken them up to the roof garden, but, to Brett's disappointment, to steps leading down to the basement and the cafeteria.

Still, just being in the building and part of the excitement thrilled Brett. The cafeteria, decorated with university pennants, portraits of old New York, blossoming plants, and student paintings, was jammed with people carrying their supper trays to the long tables. Under the noise and occasional laughter of students was some low-key rock 'n' roll. People were free to sit anywhere in the enormous dining hall. Nick led his party with their trays—Brett had chosen only a dessert of chocolate cake and ice cream—to a secluded corner, where they had a table to themselves.

"You act like you've been here before," said Michelle.

"Maybe," said Nick with a grin, looking around. "Got a few, uh, clients in this joint."

Brett said, "Clients?"

"Forget you heard that," Michelle commanded.

Josie murmured, "I'm real nervous about being here."

"What for?" asked Nick.

"People know you."

"Just eat up, will ya?" said Nick in a tone of anger.

Brett said, "One day when I'm old enough, I'll come as a student."

Leo leaned close to her face. "Yeah? You'll need thousands."

"I'll earn it. I'll work, and there're scholarships, maybe writing scholarships."

Suddenly Nick, who was sitting between Michelle and Brett, stopped eating. He shoved his plate back. His face had gone dead white and he shot a look at Leo, like a warning.

Brett jerked forward in her chair. She felt Nick's hand slipping some things into her jacket pocket. She bent to look, and Nick hissed, "Just you stay with the girls. Leo and me are . . ." He stood up.

"Going someplace?" A large, uniformed black officer, wearing security guard shoulder patches, stood at their table.

Brett was aware that the cheery noises around them had ceased as though someone had pulled a switch. All eyes were turned to their group. In the silence, with the officer standing over her, she felt terrified. Her hand went to her pocket and closed over the tiny vials that Nick had shoved there.

The officer spoke quietly but firmly.

"All of you, follow me. No fuss, please."

Leo tried to protest. "Why? We ain't done nothin'. I wanna finish my food. I paid for it. . . ."

Another security guard strolled over. He made it all seem casual. "Need any help here?"

The large man said, "No, I don't think so. Do I?" sending a piercing look at Leo.

Leo hesitated. "Nah," he said.

"Now, pick up your trays and deposit them at the counter as we leave," the large man said.

As they left the room, following the officer, Brett was aware that the noise in the hall resumed, as though the episode had never been. Back at the entrance, they were in for another shock. A city patrolman stood there, and with him the three students who had made the buy. They looked pale and shaken, the young woman no longer so self-possessed.

"Those creeps fingered us," muttered Leo.

"Shut up. Say nothing," said Nick. He, too, looked frightened.

The security guard said, "This patrolman observed what he believes was a sale."

Michelle cried, "Nick, tell them we had nothing to do with this!"

Brett spoke up boldly. "We just came for a celebration. A party for me. Because of my . . . my poem."

"How old are you, young lady?"

"Me? I'm fourteen."

The patrolman made a face. "They're getting 'em younger and younger."

The large black man turned to Nick. "No use denying the sale," he said as Nick began to protest. "The others have admitted it. In fact, they handed the stuff over to me." He held up the tiny plastic things. "What is it, anyway? Crack?"

"I dunno what you're talkin' about," said Nick, looking away. Looking directly at Brett.

Brett felt the pain attack her head. Her knees wobbled. She began to scream, "Oh, please, let me go home, I don't even know these people!"

Michelle dug into her with an elbow. "Shut it, you slob."

Brett shoved her away and pulled the vials out of her pocket. "What were these you dumped on me, Nick?" she cried.

The patrolman took them from Brett.

"You know about crack?" he asked.

"Yes. Who doesn't? I've heard about it on TV, and it's in the papers. I've been *used* by him, sir! I've never seen it before he dumped those on me, just as the guard came up. It's not fair!"

The guard looked at her, with some sadness.

"You'll have a chance to tell that to the judge. Now, all of you—move out!"

They were taken to the precinct station house in two patrol cars. They were read their rights, booked, and fingerprinted, and placed in a holding pen until the duty officer could get in touch with their various guardians. No one spoke in the holding pen. Brett sat apart, fearing Nick, who looked as though he would like to kill her.

Within the hour, the students were released to their parents and lawyers, with a date set for their court appearances. Nick and Leo were held without bail: The precinct's computer had quickly shown that they were well-known narcotics pushers.

The caseworkers for the foster home girls were called, and the girls released to them for the time being. They, too, were given dates for their court appearances.

The caseworkers escorted the girls home, and placed them under a virtual house arrest until the time of their court dates.

They were not to be trusted, they were told.

At home that night, after the workers had left, Michelle and Josie wasted no time. They beat up on Brett.

Methodically and brutally, having stuffed her mouth with a towel to stifle her cries, they beat on her face and body, tearing at her hair, scratching her, tearing her clothes, smacking her around until blood squirted from her head and mouth.

When Missus saw Brett's condition, she was terrified at the thought of calling the police; yet the cruel assault had to be reported. She helped to bathe Brett and put her to bed in her own bedroom. Then she called the caseworkers. She said that she and her husband were too old to deal with brutes and druggies; all three girls would have to leave.

"Oh, please, not again!" Brett sobbed. "It wasn't my fault. I like it here, Missus. I like my school. Don't make me change!"

"I'm sorry. I love kids, and we need the money. But it will have to be little kids, infants, in the future."

"Oh, damn you! Damn everyone! I hate you!" Brett cried.

The day that had held such dreamy promise had turned into a nightmare.

Face it, once and for all.

You know what you've become.

A throwaway.

No one's listening to you.

No one cares.

Except Mr. Taylor. But he'll be gone.

I'm too tired to think.

Wish I was dead.

10

In a crowded room of the Criminal Courts Building, where a black-robed judge sat on a high bench with a
furled American flag beside him, the group stood in silence
as the judge riffled papers and glared down at them. He was
thin-lipped, with piercing eyes and a gravelly voice that
barked orders to his court officers. They called up cases,
demanded of each person: "Raise your right hand. Do you
swear to tell the truth so help you God?" As each of Nick's
group raised a hand and swore to it, Brett felt the judge's
eyes single her out.

"Where'd you get the black eye and that swollen face,
young lady?" he demanded.

"In a fight," said Brett.

"So even after this escapade, you couldn't control yourself, could you?" the judge said angrily.

Michelle and Josie stared straight ahead. Brett made no reply.

What's the use?

No one here's going to believe me.

What's going to happen to me?

Oh, Mama, I'm so scared.

The judge was saying something to her again. "I'm going to separate your case from these older persons. Sit down for the moment."

In short order, he dispatched the others. The students, all adults, were released on their own recognizance, since none of them had records. Their college dean had suspended them for the rest of the semester, he noted, adding coldly: "If it were in my power, I'd have you privileged three paraded first before the school."

They left the courtroom with their lawyers, humiliated and cowed.

Michelle and Josie stood like penitent lambs before the judge. They let their court-appointed lawyer talk for them. He portrayed them as innocent of wrongdoing, victimized by the police who were always hauling them into court. The judge, tapping their rap sheets, said sarcastically, "Innocent, are they? Their records show they've been in and out of court on drug charges. And involved in assaults."

He stared moodily at Brett for a moment. "I'm placing them on three years' probation, with psychiatric counseling recommended."

He came down harder on the two young men, and he let

the whole court hear him: "Drug pushers are the scum of the earth," he said in a rising rage. "You've both been in this court before. This time you're going to Rikers Island prison to await trial and sentence—and I'm recommending that you get the maximum."

Leo seemed turned to jelly as he drooped and began to weep. Nick, tall and arrogant, hands dug deep in his leather jacket pockets, was trying to stare the judge down. An officer led them to the holding pen, to await the wagon that transported prisoners to Rikers Island.

"Now, young lady . . ." said the judge.

Brett got to her feet. She fixed her eyes on the wall legend high above the bench: IN GOD WE TRUST.

Dear God, don't send me to prison.

I haven't done anything.

I was framed by that creep, Nick.

Make the judge listen.

"Please, your honor," she began.

The judge cut her off. "It's your word against this, uh, Nick's. I can only speculate whether you were an accessory. But since you've never been in trouble with the courts, I'm giving you the benefit of the doubt."

"Thank you. I'd like to explain, judge . . ."

"No need. The story's in your file. All these foster homes and places you've been in. Lack of parental guidance . . ."

Leave Mama out of this.

She doesn't know. She's trying.

Why can't I explain?

Why won't you *listen* to me?

Just because I'm a kid.

He was going on. "At this moment, your caseworker is

trying to find you another foster home. I hope you appreciate what the city is doing for you. I hope this dreadful experience will never be repeated. You can sit down until your worker comes with the papers for your transfer."

The new home was on Manhattan's Upper West Side. It was a so-called experimental group home, one of several such places bought by the city for homeless adolescents, runaways, and kids rejected by their natural parents. It was programmed for independent living—preparing kids, until they reached at least their eighteenth birthday, for life on the outside.

Some dozen kids, ranging in age from fourteen to seventeen, lived cooperatively in the three-story, rehabilitated brownstone on the tree-lined street. Boys lived on the top floor; girls on the second floor; all shared in chores and preparing meals.

At the entrance, like a warning bell, a large banner told its name: SECOND-CHANCE HOUSE.

An inside wall was decorated with snapshots of graduates. The common, or living, room was spacious and homey, with comfortable chintzy couches and club chairs, a fireplace, shelves of books, a TV, an upright piano, and a glass case holding athletic trophies.

The house was staffed with round-the-clock counselors on eight-hour shifts. There was a nine o'clock curfew for younger kids, eleven o'clock for the older ones. All were required to attend school; dropouts were not tolerated, and would be transferred. Many kids held part-time jobs. All kids were on their honor to respect the house rules.

Brett was assigned to a room with bunk beds, shared with

two other girls. On her footlocker was pasted RULES & REGULATIONS. They banned noise, physical contact between residents, weapons, sexual conduct, drugs, and alcohol.

The one overwhelming feeling that Brett knew as she put her belongings in the footlocker was of being trapped.

Trapped forever in this system.

I have no say.

No one listens to what *I* want.

One thing's sure: No one cares.

Rules . . . rules . . . even though I "don't exist."

"Can I still go to my old school?" Brett asked the counselor during her initial interview.

"Back in the Village where you were in trouble, in fights?" asked the brisk, business-suited young woman. "No. I'll get you registered at your new school, nearby, on Monday. I trust you read the rules on narcotics."

"I've read them," said Brett in a sullen tone. "They don't apply to me. They don't mean nothing."

"Anything," the woman corrected. "Well, you can't deal in that here—or on the outside."

"I never have," Brett retorted.

The counselor studied her for a long moment. "You could fit in here—it was your first offense. But you'll have to change your attitude."

"All I want is to go home," said Brett.

There was a pause. Then the counselor said, gently, "You haven't been told? Your mother's very ill. Overdosed. She's at Bellevue."

Brett looked stunned. Mama in the hospital . . . sick . . . maybe dying.

"I must get to her," stammered Brett.

"All right. I'll take you there myself," the counselor said, looking at her wristwatch, "in an hour or so."

"No, now! I'm going now!" Brett cried wildly. She dashed to the door. The counselor got there before her.

"Control yourself, Brett. Don't do yourself out of another home. Let me see if one of the older girls can go with you."

She got on the public address system, which connected to all floors: "Sandy Lopez, please come to reception. At once."

Brett stood trembling, uncertain, ready to flee. In a moment, a tall girl of about seventeen, wearing an oversize sweater and blue jeans, came racing down the stairs to them.

"Sandy, do you have time from chores and homework to do us a favor?"

"Yes, ma'am."

"Brett here is a new member. She just learned that her mother is very ill at Bellevue. Would you take her there for a visit?"

"Yes, ma'am. I know the way."

"That's why I'm depending on you, Sandy."

"I understand."

"Here are subway tokens," the counselor said. "I want you both back here as soon as you leave the hospital."

"Yes, ma'am."

"Am I getting through to you, Brett?"

Brett said, echoing the other, "Yes, ma'am."

At the door, she looked back. "Thank you . . . very much, ma'am," she said in a subdued voice.

Sandy indeed knew the way. She'd been hooked on drugs, she told Brett, and spent weeks in delirium at Bellevue.

"I've been off the stuff for over two years," she said, "and if it wasn't for Miss Brownlee back there. . . ."

"The counselor?"

"Yeah, Brownie—I'd be dead. She got me the care. Stayed with the nurses. She's something! Trust her, Brett."

Brett said, "I don't trust no one. I mean, anyone."

In the six-bed dormitory, Mama didn't recognize her. She lay wide-eyed and ashen-faced, moaning softly; her arms had been taped to her sides, and her legs were strapped down.

"That's so she can't hurt herself," Sandy whispered. "She musta been scratching and tearing at her body."

Brett leaned over and kissed Mama. She asked the nurse, "Is my mama going to get well?"

The nurse said, "After a while. The question is, will she stay off the stuff after she leaves here?"

"I'll talk to her worker," said Brett.

The nurse looked hard at Brett. "Do you know why she wanted to kill herself?"

"What?"

"We think she was trying to kill herself with the overdose."

"It wasn't an accident?"

The nurse shook her head. "Maybe she needs the geography cure."

"What's that?"

"Put a continent between her and her pusher. Do you have friends in the South, or maybe on the West Coast?"

"We're . . . divorced. I'm not at home. But I do have grandparents, in California."

"Tell her worker what I think. If she wants to get well. You think about it, too."

But as soon as Mama left the hospital, she went back to her cluttered apartment. To her boyfriend.

"He saved my life, baby," she telephoned Brett. "He got the ambulance when . . . you know. He stood by me, when he could have run. I can't leave him. We love each other, baby."

"Is he a junkie, too, Mama?"

"We're clean now. Honest to God. And when I'm strong enough, I'm going to work. He knows people in the garment trade on Seventh Avenue. He's gonna get me a job modeling, he says."

"You believe that?"

"Sure. Gotta get my act together, baby," Mama said in a joking tone.

"When are you coming on a visit, Mama?"

"Soon, Brett. Take care."

11

As a place to live and feel safe, there appeared to be nothing wrong with Second-Chance House. It was a model of decent housing on the quiet block of family brownstones, with their stoops and pretty window boxes. The festering problem was within herself: Brett hated her life.

Nothing's going to stay the same.

Get lost! Who cares?

Why was this place her second chance?

Where was her first? Will there be a third?

She went to her new school feeling despair and not a little self-pity. It was within walking distance, and more than seventy percent black and Hispanic. She made no effort to make friends, chose to have her brown-bag lunch with Sandy, sitting silently with the older girls. She had come with failing grades from her previous school, except for Mr. Taylor's English class.

As often as she could, she escaped to the library, where she could be alone, feel touched, embraced even, by books. She came to know the librarian better than her teachers.

One idea now took root. When she couldn't bear it anymore, she would run away. Not to Mama and her boyfriend. Back to Mister and Missus. She would go down on her knees and plead with them to let her stay. She would never give them any more trouble. She would work for them. They could even adopt her if they wanted to. And she'd go back to Mr. Taylor's class.

The fantasy, with no real shape at first, haunted her studies and her sleep. She did her chores like the others, sat quietly at meals in the common dining room, listening to the chatter, distancing herself from everyone but Sandy. Privately, she was only biding her time, until she ran.

In the third week of Brett's transfer to Second-Chance House, her life took a dramatic turn. The fantasy began to fade. Her life seemed to stop spinning her about, and took on real meaning.

Two brothers had been transferred in by the court: Malcolm, a fourteen-year-old, darkly handsome, stocky boy with a brashly confident manner and sporting a big green metal button on his denim jacket which said, Kiss Me, I'm Irish. And Petey, ten years old, as unlike Malcolm as he could be, with his slight frame, pale, thin face, and tentative smiles. He stayed close to his older brother, and nodded eagerly as

Malcolm announced to Brownie, "We have to room together, you know."

Brownie began to demur. "I think he's too young for this house. Normally, we take only adolescents."

"We can't be separated," Malcolm said flatly. "No way. I mean, the court said, 'No way.' "

Brownie said, amused, "Did it now?"

"Yes, ma'am."

"Like you didn't lay it on the judge?"

"Didn't have to, ma'am," he said, looking very angelic. He had Petey's hand in a hard grip.

"Well, perhaps we can make an exception," Brownie said, "since you're brothers. We don't like to separate siblings."

"Hey, sibling," said Malcolm, "you hear the lady?"

She started to ruffle Petey's hair. The boy stiffened, and moved away.

Brett, witnessing the episode, felt a rush of affection for them, fascinated by the protectiveness of the older boy. Like a father, she thought. To her surprise, she found herself talking to them quite freely at suppertime. Seating herself next to Petey, she told them, "I have a brother about Petey's age."

"Oh, yeah?" said Malcolm. "Where is he?"

"I'm . . . not sure. We've never met."

Malcolm said, matter-of-factly, "Divorce?"

"Right, Malcolm."

He said abruptly, "Call me Mac. Everyone does. I hate the name Malcolm."

He seemed so down-to-earth, sophisticated, straightforward. She watched TV with them that evening, feeling like a member of a family. After Mac sent Petey up to bed, she told him she'd written a poem about divorce.

"Read it to me," he said. "That's one subject I'm an authority on. My father's twice divorced. His name's Malcolm . . . not mine, though."

Brett got out her notebook, and did as he said. As she read, she felt a flash of happiness, as though she had found a soul mate.

"Hey, that's not too shabby," he said.

Brett pointed to the large green button. "Do you mean that?" She was startled at her own boldness.

He laughed. "Nah. An ego thing. I bought it on Saint Patrick's Day and people laugh at it so much, I always wear it."

"Has anyone actually, you know . . . ?"

"Kissed me?"

"Well, yes."

He roared with laughter. "Millions!" He added swiftly, "Nah. It's just for fun."

He pulled a bunch of buttons from his jacket pocket. "Wanna see some more? This one's another favorite." The button read: Ask Me Anything / I Don't Byte.

Malcolm said, "I hope they've got computers at this school."

"Just one," said Brett. "Too poor."

She read the other mottoes: Inside, State of Frenzy; Find Yourself; Hi, Hi, Hi, Hi!

Malcolm said, "Hey, I'm gonna give you this one. You're kinda shy. Watch people say it back to you." He pinned the Hi, Hi button to her shirt.

Brett said, "Hey, thanks." At the boy's gift and his touch, she felt again the flash of happiness. The others glanced at them curiously before going back to the TV.

Next day before supper, Brownie announced she had obtained complimentary tickets to a Saturday matinee performance of a wonderful pop opera at Lincoln Center, Bertolt Brecht's play, *The Threepenny Opera,* with music by Kurt Weill. There were some groans around the table. "Opera!" Brownie said, "I think you'll be pleasantly surprised. It's not grand opera, though I hope to get tickets for that sometime. It's a parody—a fanciful story, set to music, about beggars and thieves living in London's criminal districts."

Her audience grew quiet at that.

"Actually, this show began as *The Beggar's Opera* back in the 1700s, by a writer called John Gay, who was concerned about the misery all around him. The hero of the show decides to capitalize on the misery by making quite healthy people look like cripples, wearing rags and using crutches; and he sends them out to beg. They get profits from the wealthy." Broad smiles all around. "He has one enemy, however: a well-dressed rogue named MacHeath, who's a friend of the sheriff of London."

Mac sat up straight at the name. Petey grinned at him.

"This MacHeath has his own gang, preying on the wealthy; only Mac also manages to woo and marry the hero's daughter, Polly."

"Go on," said Mac.

"It all ends well. There's a grand finale, and MacHeath is saved from the gallows."

Mac said, "Hey, that's some story. Put us down for two tickets, ma'am."

"Well, I'm not sure that Petey . . ." Brownie began.

"He goes where I go. Anyway, like you said, it's fanciful, ain't it?"

"Well, yes."

"And a ticket for Polly here," he added mischievously. "I mean Brett."

There was laughter at Mac's crack, as other hands shot up to be included.

On matinee day, Brownie bundled them into her Ford station wagon and drove to the State Theater at Lincoln Center. None had ever seen live theater before. Brett thrilled to the crowds of people pouring into the elegant, chandeliered showplace. Brownie had got them good seats in the balcony, with panoramic views of the musical drama and the orchestra in the pit. Brett sat between Mac and Petey.

As the great hall darkened, the show opened with men and women in rags begging and thieves stealing and carousing to the stirring music. Mac's hand was on Brett's arm as he listened tensely to the solo about Mac-the-Knife.

It described how Mac had a knife, but he kept it hidden. At the close of the ballad, the Narrator proclaimed that the businessman, J. Peachum, put his followers in rags and tatters, and sent them begging to test the indifference of mankind.

Now the entire orchestra swelled with compassion, and *The Threepenny Opera* was on its mesmerizing way. For over two hours, Brownie and the Second-Chance-House kids sat captivated. At intermission, she treated them to cold drinks on the mezzanine floor. No doubt about it: Her choice of theater and show was a hit; they could identify with the characters onstage, and appreciate the satire. She bought them the record so they could remember the music.

On the drive home, Mac announced, "From now on, everybody, I'm Mac-the-Knife. He's got brains."

"Also weapons," said Brett.

Brownie asked casually, "You ever used a knife?"

"Well, once," said Mac. "When I threatened my old man with a dinner knife."

"You wouldn't have . . ." Petey began softly.

"He was beating Petey because the kid said he hated vegetables and threw the plate on the floor. He was only five then. That dumb wife was yelling at Petey, telling my father to smack him one for her, and I couldn't stand it."

"But the knife . . .?"

"I dunno. I was sure threatening him, and if they didn't leave off beating on Petey, I . . . might have used it. Right, Petey?"

The small boy nodded, his face gone grim.

"That was when they threw us out. She told the judge she was afraid of us. Of me!"

"Didn't the judge ask you . . .?" Brownie began.

"You kiddin'? Judges don't listen to us."

"I know," said Brett.

"We were country kids, living in a small town in Maryland, and she was our second stepmother. They began to ship us around, one place to another. At least they never tried to separate us."

"Who's 'they'?"

"The judges . . . the workers. One town to another."

"And after?" asked Brett.

"Here—New York, where we had an aunt. She was nice but about a hundred, and we were too much for her, I guess. So out we went again."

Brownie drove silently, brooding on his tale. Mac turned to her with his mischievous grin. "Anyway, Petey didn't like her vegetables, either."

They laughed at his small joke. And Petey said, earnestly, "I try to eat everything now."

"Good boy," said Brownie.

12

In Sioux Falls, South Dakota, Charlotte was no longer just singing about "California Dreamin'." Her dream was about to become reality. The Jaysons were packing up.

Charlotte had long pestered her husband to put in for a transfer to the West Coast branch of his firm. It had not been an easy time for him. "We can have a permanent house there, maybe with palms and orange trees," she had argued. "I'll get a job—secretaries are always in demand—and we'll have two salaries coming in. And," she added her clincher, "Tommy can really get to know his grandparents. You want that, don't you?"

Brett said, "You've had your heart set on this move."

"Right!"

"But we're settled here, Charlotte, and I'm due for a big promotion, as you know."

"So get 'em to promote you to Los Angeles, or some place near Carson Heights, where your parents live."

"You really want this . . . uprooting?"

"I really want this."

"Right now, when I'm on my way up?"

"What about me?" Her voice was rising. "There's another reason, maybe the all-important reason."

"Oh?"

Charlotte plunged on. "We had an agreement when we got married. To be our own entity? No other life before ours? Well, I won't be satisfied until I put the whole country between us and them."

"You think such a move will wipe 'them' off the earth?"

"I sure do!" she snapped.

He stared at her, fearing another of her outbursts, with the boy doing his homework near them.

He said, backing off, "I'm not sure I can swing the transfer."

"So try," she commanded.

Tommy had looked up from his work, listening, wiping off his glasses. He also knew better than to argue with his mother, but he was tearful at the thought of impending change and loss of friends.

The arguments had receded as Brett arranged for his transfer; he rationalized that peace in the family would be worth it. With chagrin, he remembered the storm he'd had to ride out at home because of a phone call he'd accepted in his office from some strange foster parent in New York: "Your daughter calls me Missus, and it's all the name you need," the woman had said by way of introduction. He had felt the old stab of guilt at the word *daughter*.

The woman went on, "She's been in trouble with the courts, a drug-related problem. Her mother's ill. I can't contend with this in my home any longer." The woman's voice was gentle, worried.

He said, "You don't understand my present family situation. . . ."

"I understand this," said Missus. "The judge says you're abdicating your responsibilities. We feel Brett needs her father."

Brett! His namesake! The daughter he'd given up . . . no, been forced to forget.

He said heavily, "I'll talk it over with my wife. What's your number?"

When after a couple of days he told Charlotte about the call, she raged that he'd accepted it in the first place. What he'd done was a violation of their marriage commitment. The girl didn't exist for them!

Charlotte's barrage and naked jealousy, once again revealing that she couldn't bear to think he'd loved anyone before her, stunned him anew. He had fled to a neighborhood bar, returning home after midnight, and slept in Tommy's room on the spare cot rather than deal with her wrath again that night.

He never returned the New York call.

He told himself that the judge had a point, but not in this case. Wasn't young Brett better off, far from Charlotte? The past was dead, he told himself. In the same mood, he chose not to fight his wife's campaign to move the family to California. Anyway, he was longing for a real reunion with his aging parents.

The transfer was to the small town of San Vision, a few miles from Carson Heights. Brett's firm, it turned out, was not too displeased with his idea of developing its Far Western branch. The town of fifty thousand had a fine full range of industrial and agricultural services, but its commercial potential was not being realized. Brett would join a stable work force, and be expected, in time, to effect a fully computerized system, linking it to branches in Los Angeles and San Francisco. For his part, Brett was proud of the trust placed in him, and began to welcome the challenge.

Charlotte was happiest. She had collected literature about the new location, and delighted in quoting from the advertisements on how "living was at its best" where they were going: two national parks at their door, Kings Canyon and Sequoia; water sports, fishing, boating; good schools.

She flew to the Coast ahead of them. Within a week, she had put a down payment on a house "just minutes from the plant," she phoned Brett. And, she exulted, "It's on a real palm-lined street, with built-ins and a den for your workshop. Well, the town's not called San Vision for nothing—it's got vision to spare for us, right?"

Her fervor touched Brett sufficiently for him to ask mildly whether Gram could help with . . .

Charlotte cut him off. "I'll see them when you and Tommy come. I don't want any interference. We'll ship out most of our things, get settled that way much faster than if we buy new stuff here."

She was shrill again. Privately, he could guess what she meant by no interference. He sighed. Gram, with her gentle, intelligent outlook on life, and T.J., bighearted, trusting, compassionate, would recoil from such an implication. What they both did share was a keen sense of duty. Was that perhaps what Charlotte—and he himself—really feared as they met his parents?

In fact, they brushed up against that almost at once. Gram had prepared a welcoming dinner, the festive table adorned with yellow roses from her garden. Dessert was a home-baked chocolate cake decorated with *Charlotte, Brett, Tommy* on top. The reunion bubbled with loving questions, and once Tommy left his place to run and hug Gram and T.J.

"Wonderful to have you living so close to us at last," Gram said. "Especially at this time of our lives."

"What do you mean?" Brett joked. "You always said you'd never leave age thirty-nine! You promised!"

"That's right," retorted his father. "For thirty years, we stayed at thirty-nine!"

They laughed, and raised their wineglasses to toast that. They talked about Brett's new job and Tommy's new school, and made plans for the elder Jaysons to visit their son in San Vision. As they rose to leave, Brett felt it was the happiest of times. Until his mother posed her question. It was casual, but it dropped with the impact of a bomb, shattering the mood.

"Will young Brett be coming, too?" Gram asked.

In the sudden silence, Brett stared at Charlotte, and Tommy asked, "Young Brett?"

90

Charlotte said coldly, "There is no such person in our lives."

T.J. said, "What on earth do you mean?"

"Just that. I thought it was explained to you long ago."

Gram told Tommy, "We're talking about our granddaughter, Brett." She kept her tone light, striving to restore calm.

Charlotte said, "We must be going. Tommy has a lot of preparation to do for school. And, uh, just one more thing," she went on, ignoring Tommy's questioning look. "I think it should be understood at once: We never even mention her name. She doesn't exist for us."

"That may be," said T.J. evenly. "But she's mentioned here, and she's certainly not forgotten. That should be understood, too."

Gram put in, "Now, then, let's just postpone all this talk for another time, shall we?"

"There will be no other time," said Charlotte, her tone grim, forbidding. "Don't you agree, Brett?"

Brett moved to the door, his arm around Tommy. "Let's go," he said abruptly. "Thanks for everything, Mom, Dad. See you soon, okay?"

On the drive back to San Vision and their new home, Charlotte held her tongue because of Tommy's presence. Once he was in bed and out of earshot, she turned on Brett bitterly.

"Why didn't you back me up?"

"They got the message without any help from me."

"Your mother did it purposely!"

"Mom isn't like that."

"I told you once; I'm telling you again. I won't stand for any interference in our lives."

"That's pretty clear, to everyone."

"Damn right!"

For a moment, he found his nerve. "So get off my back."

His tone surprised her, warned her against further argument.

But both knew in their hearts that the matter of young Brett was far from over.

13

Mac and Petey were the ones who made Second-Chance House tolerable to Brett. Because of them, because she wanted to stay near the brothers, she tried to cooperate.

She did her chores without complaint. She sat, passively to be sure, in the counseling sessions, listening to the others without involving herself—that is, unless Mac pepped things up with some irreverent crack. Like how he tried to save on carfares. Once he tried to sneak Petey on the bus without paying for him. When the bus driver said, "Where's his fare, he's more than five," Mac retorted, "Nah, he just looks older because he worries all the time!" That broke everyone up, even Brownie.

She loved the way Mac cared for his brother. She thought about her own half brother and yearned for someone like Petey to share things with.

Mama said his name once.

Tommy.

I wonder if he knows about me.

Well, one thing's sure: Kids don't stay kids.

They grow up, have minds of their own.

When we meet, I'll say simply: I'm Brett. Your big sister, Tommy.

She wished she had a picture of him. Did he look like their father? Who were his friends? Did he like to write the way she did? Did that run in families?

Mama came once on a visit, with a new friend. She had lost more weight, and Brett told her sadly she looked like skin and bones. Mama's once lovely eyes, enormous in the bony face, were bloodshot and darkly ringed. Mama seemed even to have shrunk. Could drugs and booze do that to a person? Brett wondered. Mama's smile seemed to plead as she said, "I'm sorry it took so long to get here, baby. I had a relapse. Kingman here—everyone calls him King—he took care of me."

The man towered over them. He was a heavy-set six-footer with crew cut hair, wearing designer jeans, denim jacket, and triple gold chains around his neck. He looked young enough to be Mama's son.

What number is King, Mama?

King . . . yuck!

How long this time, Mama?

Is he using or dealing or both?

Oh, Mama, where're you heading now?

Mama was saying, "I've got news for you, baby. King would like you to come home with us. He wants to make us a family. What do you say to that?"

Brett was well aware that King was staring at her appraisingly.

"I don't know, Mama."

"You could take care of me, you know. You're old enough now."

Brett stammered, "I'd have to change schools, and . . . I've got friends here."

"Well, friends don't come before family, do they?"

Brett burst out, afraid, "You're not married . . . or anything?"

For the first time, King spoke. His voice was lazy, patronizing, the voice of someone used to taking charge. "Is that any way to speak to your mother? She wants you to come home."

"After nine, ten years!" cried Brett. She felt confused. How many times had she pleaded to go home? Now . . . ?

"I'll have to talk it over with my counselor."

The man persisted. "Don't you love your mother?"

"Oh, come on, King," Mama protested weakly.

Brett said, "I love you, Mama. But I can't just walk away from here. What if it doesn't work out for us? Don't you know the name of this house? It's called Second-Chance. I'm on *probation* here."

Her emphasis seemed to wake Mama up. She said hurriedly, "Well, you talk it over with your counselor—what's her name?"

"Miss Brownlee—Brownie."

King said in a harsh voice, "I thought we came to take her back with us."

"King, it's not that simple," Mama said. "See, she's been placed here. On, uh, probation. It's up to this worker, I guess, whether she can leave."

"You can't say I didn't make a generous offer," said King, turning away.

Mama gave Brett a hug and started after him, stumbling over her parting words, "Now you talk to this, uh, Brownie and, uh, let me—let us know, Brett."

"Are they married?" asked Brownie.

"No, ma'am. She said he was her friend."

"How do you feel about that?"

"I think, even if they was married . . ."

"Were . . ."

". . . were married, I wouldn't go."

"Why not?"

"I don't know. I think he may be a druggie, too. He reminded me of Nick. And anyway, I didn't like the way he looked me over."

Brownie stared at her for a long moment. "You're growing up, Brett."

"He scared me. I used to hide from those other friends of Mama's when I was a little kid."

"I understand."

"I'd like to be with my mama. But not this way. I'd be afraid all the time."

"Relax, Brett. It's all right. There's no way I'd recommend breaking up your life here under such conditions."

"Thank you, ma'am."

After the encounter with Mama and King, Brett was more satisfied with life at the house. She was pleased when Brownie corrected her English, for, as the counselor put it, "If you want to write good poetry, you have to write and speak good English."

At school, however, she remained a loner. In study hall periods, she found herself writing poems instead of doing her assignments. (She could never forget Mr. Taylor's confidence in her talent. It was her goad and inspiration.) Still, her grades were improving, and Sandy often helped with her homework.

Brownie arranged picnics in Central Park. And Mac, captaining the softball team, always chose her for his side. She was deeply affected by her friendship with the brothers, not afraid to share confidences with Mac. She told him about her encounter with Mama and King, and Brownie's decision.

Mac whistled. "Whew! You did right!"

"But are we never going to be able to go home?"

"Petey and me—we ain't got no home."

"Haven't got any home," Brett corrected him gently.

"Yeah. Hey, you sound like Brownie!"

Brett said, "Petey's so little. Have you ever thought about getting adopted?"

Mac said, "Sure, lotsa times. But only if we go together."

Brownie wrote Mama that Brett was Brownie's ward; that under the law, Brett had to serve her probation at Second-Chance House, so she could not then return home.

However, she wrote, Mama could visit often. In fact, she

hoped Mama would come for the family counseling sessions, to help herself as well as Brett.

Mama never came to the house again. Perhaps it was her way of placating her friend.

Mama seemed, Brett thought bitterly, to have vanished from the earth. In a down mood, she wrote a poem about how she saw herself, in a sort of mocking purge:

> I see myself an outsider,
> Lost to those who went before,
> Still I look about for strength,
> To batter down the door.
>
> I see myself as . . . nobody,
> And thirst just to belong,
> It's like talking to the wind.
> Who's listening to my song?
>
> Talking to the cruel wind,
> I acknowledge in my soul:
> It's plain—I'm an outsider,
> Some being not quite whole.
>
> Still, there I knock at the door,
> "Please, let me in," I say.
> I'm talking to the cruel wind,
> And turn brimming eyes away.

She worked on the poem for a long time, changing words, correcting lines, keenly remembering Mr. Taylor's confidence in her. She called her poetic reflections "Talking to the Wind."

Later, she showed her poem to Mac and Petey. Mac praised it, but he looked rather hurt.

"Hey, what's all this about 'outsider'?" he asked. "There's us three and there's Sandy and Brownie . . . we're practically family. Aren't we?" He nudged his brother.

Petey said, "Sure."

"Then show it. Give her a kiss."

Petey grinned, and he shyly kissed Brett's cheek.

Brett hugged the boy. "That's a big wow!"

The moment triggered something else in Mac. " 'Talking to the Wind,' " he reflected. "Maybe we are. But don't forget I'm Mac-the-Knife," he boasted. "That means I'm your protector as well as Petey's."

She laughed. "I won't forget."

He went to Shakespeare & Co. Booksellers on Broadway next day, and asked a collegiate-looking salesman to suggest a good book of poetry, paperback, secondhand. He had a dollar left from the allowance that all kids at the house got for their chores.

The young man rummaged around in a box labeled Special Sales, Reduced and came up with what he called one of the grandest books ever written. It was a well-worn copy of *Sonnets from the Portuguese,* by Elizabeth Barrett Browning, only ninety cents.

"Your girlfriend will love this," the man said.

Mac said crossly, "How d'ya know it's for a girl?"

The man laughed in a friendly way. "Wild guess."

Brett was thrilled with her present. Mac inscribed the inside cover page, *To my friend, Brett-the-Poet.* He signed with a flourish, *From Mac-the-Knife.*

In the school library, she read up on the strange, secretly romantic life of the poet; of how ill Elizabeth Barrett had been since age fifteen, and of her despotic father, against whom she finally rebelled in order to marry Robert Browning. The love poems stirred her, and made her feel at one with the poet—and with Mac.

Then, two days later, the world she had at last begun to feel attuned to crashed in on her. It started with a simple enough adventure.

14

The handsome new bicycle of the kid next door stood like a beckoning sentinel against his stoop. For some reason, the front wheel had not been removed for security, nor was the bike chained to the garden rail. Mac had marveled at the bike more than once, in fact, drooled over its soft, cushioned saddle, whitewall tires, and upright handlebars.

"That's a real hotshot bike," Mac told Brett admiringly as they returned from school. "Musta cost a fortune. An' he leaves it just standing there for anyone to take. Whatta creep."

"He must have gone in his house for a minute," said Brett. "Took a chance."

Mac ran his hand over the lustrous leather and handlebars. Enviously.

"Hey, Brett, wanna go for a spin?" he said.

"What? Mac, you wouldn't . . .!"

"A quick one."

"I've never been on a bike before."

"Piece o' cake."

"Suppose he comes down and finds it gone."

"We'll watch for that."

Even as he spoke, Mac had wheeled the bicycle to the street, and showed Brett how to sit and hold on behind him. They took off shakily, then Mac gathered speed, standing straight up on the pedals while Brett, her arms around him, held him tight. The rush of wind, the speed, the danger of being found out excited and frightened her.

"Let's go back now, Mac."

"Hey, going great. One more block . . ."

"No, please!"

But Mac was heading for the next block. Then a third. Reluctantly, at Brett's pleading, he started to make a U-turn to go back when disaster struck. He saw a car speeding from the opposite direction and lost control. He ran the bike up on the sidewalk and into a brick wall. The crash threw both of them to the pavement, the machine falling with a mighty noise.

"You hurt, Brett?"

"I think I'll live. My forehead and my wrist are bleeding. But look at the bike," she said in horror. The bicycle lay sprawled on its side like a wounded animal. The whole front was a mess. As they stood it up, they saw that several wire spokes were also twisted out of shape.

"Cripes," muttered Mac, "did I do that?"

They walked the damaged bike back in silence. Waiting at their destination was not only the kid next door but also his father. He was a heavy-set, bearded man in his shirtsleeves and dungarees who looked like a wrestler. When he saw the condition of the bike, he yelled curses at Mac and Brett.

"Thieves, robbers! I've called the police. They'll know how to deal with you!"

Brett began, "I'm sorry. We only . . ."

Mac muttered, "Why call the cops? I'll pay."

"Oh, yeah? I'm gonna get that house closed down, you hear. Completely. Goddamn juvenile delinquents, the lot of you!"

He moved threateningly toward Mac. "I'd like to take a swipe at you now!" he said, raising his arm.

Brett screamed and ran between them, shoving at the man with all her strength, screaming, "Leave him alone, you bastard!"

Then Mac was yelling, "Don't hurt her!"

The man fell back. "Yeah, let the cops handle this."

Brownie took the episode very hard.

"What you did reflects on the whole house, and puts us all at risk," she told them. "That man has filed several complaints against us already; now he has a real case."

"Can't we apologize and pay for the damage?" asked Brett. The thrill of the adventure was drained from her. She was hurting, emotionally as well as physically.

Mac muttered, "What can he do anyway?"

"Plenty. He's not only got you charged with theft and property damage, but he's also accusing us—the house—

of lack of discipline, of being a threat to the street. Oh, Mac, Brett, how could you?"

Brownie stared at them, weary and disgusted.

To Brett, the Family Court with its uniformed attendants and high bench was like a replay of her earlier disgrace. Who would listen to them here? It would, once more, be like talking to the wind, an outsider again. The officers seemed like clones of one another: men and women in the same neat white shirts, black ties, black trousers, shoulder badges. As cases were called, she heard again the strange intoning: "Do you swear to tell the truth, so help you God?" Where was God in this place?

There did seem to be one big difference, she suddenly realized: the judge.

He swept in from the robing room, a brisk, sandy-haired, slight man, his loose black robe barely covering his tieless shirt as he sat in the high-backed green leather chair. He swung in it, back and forth, listening to the preliminaries, but mostly to the people.

There were several cases before Second-Chance House.

There was Joseph, a frightened, thin boy of twelve, in a white T-shirt, red corduroys, and sneakers, sitting beside a large, stout woman. Her eyes were fixed pleadingly on the judge.

"You're Joseph's guardian, his grandmother?"

"Yes, your honor."

"Where is Joseph's mother?"

"She's, uh, in prison, sir."

Joseph seemed to sink deep in his seat.

"The file here," the judge said, tapping the folder before

him, "shows you've been using cocaine. That's why the worker brought you in. Are you using?"

"Oh, no, sir. Absolutely not, your honor."

"Or pot?"

"No, sir. I only smoke Marlboros."

The judge sent her a long, amused look. Then he turned to Joseph. "I want you to understand that what *you* say is important to me, Joseph. My name is Judge Bernard Leland. You know I'm your friend, don't you?"

Joseph nodded but looked confused.

"You come along with me, Joseph." He motioned to the boy's worker and a court officer, led them to the small robing room behind the bench, and closed the door. They remained there for about ten minutes, while those in the courtroom sat in hushed silence, waiting. When they returned, the judge to his bench, the boy to his grandmother, the judge said, "Feel better, Joseph?"

The boy smiled and looked happy.

"Tell Grandma what I asked you."

The boy told her, "He asked if I wanted to go to a foster home."

"And what did you say to me?" the judge asked.

"I said no, I'm afraid."

"And what did I tell you, Joseph?"

"That you won't take me away from Grandma."

That lady gave Joseph a big hug.

The judge said, "He wants to stay with you, ma'am. I won't take him away from you. But the way you've been living is troubling us here." She leaned forward, trembling. "Now the worker tells me Joseph has two brothers in care, and he wants more than anything to see them. So I'm requesting the sibling visits. Do you understand, ma'am?"

"Oh, yes, I do, your honor." They left together.

The judge wrote in the file, and asked the worker for a report in two months. "Call the next case."

There were a couple of cases where the guardians of minors had not shown up, and the judge issued warrants for their arrest. Then there was sixteen-year-old Mary Beth. She had been living for three years in a group home. Her mother beside her, was in sharp contrast to Mary Beth's drab appearance: She was a well-tailored woman in pink satin blouse and pants suit, fingering a rope of pearls.

The judge asked, "Why did you place Mary Beth in care all these years?"

"Because I had no partner, no space, and she was having these seizures all the time."

"How is the child doing in care?" he asked the caseworker.

"She's adjusting, your honor."

"And you, Mary Beth? I want to hear from you."

"Well, it's okay with me," the girl said with a shrug. "She keeps having all these . . . partners."

Brett, listening closely, shuddered. It was as though the question had been directed to her, too.

The judge wrote rapidly in the girl's file, saying, "Petition granted to keep Mary Beth in the group home."

Now it was Brett's and Mac's turn. They went before the judge with Brownie at their side, as the clerk read the charges against them and Second-Chance House. The judge said, "I want to hear what you kids have to say. You first, Brett. Tell me how you're doing in the house."

Brett gulped. This judge sounded concerned. "I'm doing fine, sir."

"Why aren't your parents here?"

"My mother's ill. And I haven't seen or heard from my father since I was . . . very young. He's in some other state."

"And you, Malcolm?" asked the judge.

Mac started at the sound of his name. "Ain't got no parents to speak of, sir. I take care of my brother, Petey. I'm sorry, sir, about . . ."

"We'll get to that—all in good time. Now, you've seen how I listen to the kids themselves in this court. Kids are important to me. Follow me."

As before, he led them, Brownie, and a court officer to his robing room.

"Don't get the wrong idea," he said as he eased himself into the straight wooden chair behind his desk. "I'm not condoning what you kids did; it was shameful, criminal. But what I really want to know is how I can work with you to do better with your lives."

Mac stared at him, then whispered an aside to Brett.

"Something secret, Malcolm?"

"Mac, sir, please."

"All right, Mac. Want to tell me?"

Mac looked sheepish. "I only said, 'This judge is cool.'"

Judge Leland looked pleased. "I'll take that as a compliment, son."

It was Mac's turn to look pleased. "Ain't no one called me that as long as I can remember."

"When you kids come into my court," the judge said evenly, "you're all my sons and daughters. That's what I meant by saying we should work together, to do better."

He turned to Brownie. "You've been in my court before, representing kids. You know how angry I can get about the abdication of responsibility by parents." He sighed and went on. "Now, back to these charges."

Brownie said, "Mac and Brett want to make it up to the youngster who owns the bike. They'll do anything. . . ."

The judge said, "That's only the short end of the stick." They all waited in agony for what might come. "Forget the charges against the house," the judge went on. "The file tells me volumes about the good work you and your colleagues have been doing, Miss Brownlee. Nothing's going to happen to the house. In fact, I wish the city could fund more such houses for kids in trouble, for kids discarded by parents and guardians."

"Right on, judge," Mac burst out boldly.

"I don't usually let people sit in my court while other cases are being heard," the judge said, "but I bent the rules for you two kids today, so you could listen to what's happening to others, and not feel unique. Now, Brett, I've been studying your file. I see you've been in care for, let me see. . . ."

"Over nine years, sir," Brett said quietly.

"Your mother's sick, an addict. She'll need help for some time to come. But your father's conduct is plain disgraceful," he said in a hard tone. "I wish I had *him* in my court today, give him what's due him. But let me go on, Brett. You do have grandparents in California . . . ?"

"But I don't know them, sir," she burst out. "And I do have friends—good friends—at Second-Chance House, and Brownie . . ." Her voice trailed off, afraid.

Mama, what am I saying?

Mama, what am I to do?

I wanted to stay near you, help you, but you're never here.

"Listen to me, Brett. I like to keep families together. These grandparents—your father's parents—have shown, according to this file, they're concerned about you. They care about you. Now, I'm going to ask Miss Brownlee to phone them; tell them that you've been in trouble again, and this judge is recommending that they take responsibility at this critical time of your life. At least, give it a try, Brett. Miss Brownlee, will you do that for me?"

"Will do, your honor," said Brownie.

And suddenly, it was as though Judge Bernard Leland had found his audience. He rolled on passionately: "I've seen scores of kids like you in foster care who never should be in certain foster homes, or group homes. You kids happen to be in a good one.

"I myself have seen horrible conditions in some of these places," he went on. "Kids have a right to be heard. Too many become victims of the system that's supposed to be protecting them.

"Now, as for you, son," he continued, "your devotion to young Petey is exemplary. I'm going to let you work out with Miss Brownlee how to make apologies and restitution for the damage."

"Hey, thank you, your honor."

The house threw a party for Brett the day before she was to leave for Carson Heights and her grandparents' home. The living room was festooned with colored balloons. Mac and Petey baked her a frosted apple pie, and Mac stuck his favorite button on top: Kiss Me, I'm Irish. Everyone applauded when Petey carried the pie in on a huge platter, and the kids yelled, "You've gotta do it, Brett!"

She laughed, and kissed both Petey and Mac, then pocketed the button. "I'll keep this pinned to my heart," she said.

Brownie drove her to the airport the next day. She reminded Brett that her grandfather would meet her at the Los Angeles airport for the drive to Carson Heights. He would be, he had told Brownie, carrying a bunch of red roses so she would recognize him.

"Everything's going to come up roses now," Brownie assured her, as they kissed and said good-bye. "Believe it. Stay in touch."

"Oh, I will, I will," Brett promised fervently.

Good-bye, Sandy and Mac and Petey.

I'll never forget you.

I miss you already.

Good-bye, Mama—for a while.

Dear God, take care of Mama.

Part Two

. . . love that comes too late,
Like a remorseful pardon
slowly carried . . .

William Shakespeare,
ALL'S WELL THAT ENDS WELL
Act 5, Scene 3

15

It was cold, with threatening skies in the New York cemetery, and the plain pinewood coffin bearing Mac seemed drear and lonely. Brett could hear what others were telling her, but only with one part of her mind. The other part was crying helplessly for forgiveness.

Why didn't I guess how you were hurting, Mac?

Why didn't I write more often?

You could have phoned—talked to me!

I could have helped, somehow.

Forgive me. Please forgive me.

How strange—that with a flourish of his pen, one judge had changed the pattern of her life for the better. While with the flourish of another judge's pen, the pattern of Mac's life had been changed for the worse.

"From the moment they separated him from Petey,"
Brownie was murmuring, as she wept, "Mac seemed to give
up, not to care anymore. I think he stole things to get attention, to get punished. When he didn't feel punished enough,
he took it on himself to do it . . . this way. To end his pain."

Brett's arm was around Petey. "I had to sneak away to
see my brother," Petey said brokenly. "My adoptive parents
kept saying he was a bad influence. They always tried to stop
me, even from phoning."

And Judge Leland, standing with the Second-Chance
House kids, said with quiet anger, "I would never have
separated the boys. The Adoption Services probably guessed
that, and saw that Petey's case came up in another court. I'm
heartbroken over this, Brett."

Brett became aware that the minister was asking her to
say her poem now. She stilled her tears and steadied her
voice as she said the poem that Mac had asked for: "Talking
to the Wind."

"How old were you when you wrote that poem?" Judge
Leland asked her as he drove them back to the house.

"About fourteen, I guess," said Brett.

"And are you yourself still talking to the wind? I mean, I
have in mind your own brother. Have you met him yet?"

"No, sir. It's not allowed."

"Not allowed!" he fairly shouted. "You're seventeen
now, child. Who's to keep you kids from meeting, getting to
know each other, and stop all this talking to the wind?"

"They don't want me to interfere."

"Who are 'they'?"

"Well, my father and his wife—they're living in the town

next to ours." She went on bitterly, "It's really that . . . wife of his. She's got this law she's invented to keep me out of their lives, insists Mama and I don't exist."

The judge said, calm and deliberate now, "Listen to me, Brett. We're all shaken up by this day and what drives people to punish themselves so cruelly. But what are we to learn from it? Not to be afraid to trust our best instincts. Don't you think, Brett, that brother of yours is as curious about you as you are about him? Maybe you need each other. Don't you think you have a right to know each other?"

"Yes. But I don't want to hurt my grandparents."

"Do they have to know?"

"Oh, I couldn't go behind their backs, sir. I love them. I've never done anything I couldn't tell them about."

"Well, has it occurred to you, young lady," the judge went on sharply, "that they're waiting for you yourself to make the move? That perhaps more than ever, after this sad journey of yours, you should act?"

Brett pondered his words. "I'll think about it."

Brownie put in quietly, "Brett is staying at the house tonight, judge. We'll talk about it."

"You do that," the judge said. "And you, Brett—go for it!"

16

Brett had never been in the town of San Vision, California. Out of deference to her grandparents, she had always turned back when she reached the part of the expressway that separated the two towns. Now, for the first time, she biked on, crossing the palm-lined border to what she had thought of as the frontier, and rode into San Vision.

She was not surprised to find it was much like Carson Heights, with its pleasant interior of landscaped, low-slung houses, blossoming hedges, and open driveways. In the late morning, she rode for several blocks, trying on her own to find the school. But the streets were deserted, and she realized she'd have to ride up to one of the houses to ask directions.

Suddenly, ahead of her she saw another cyclist slowly pedaling his way; actually, reading something in his hand as he pedaled. She put on speed and caught up with him.

"I'm looking for the middle school," she called over, as she rode alongside. "Can you point me in that direction, please?"

The young man smiled. "I can do better than that. I'm going there myself."

"Hey, that's great."

"Meeting someone there?"

"Well . . . my brother."

"My sister's in the middle school," he said. "I'm taking her this book, which she forgot. Cripes, it's a long time since I read *Treasure Island*."

"How old is your sister?"

"Lucy? She's fourteen, going on twenty-one!"

"That bright?"

They laughed together, as they rode side by side, and Brett felt easy in his company. He was tall and lanky, with streaky brown hair and wide-set, candid brown eyes that invited open talk. He wore a UCLA-lettered sweater, and volunteered, noting her look, "I'm not there yet. But I've been accepted. Starting next February."

"Congratulations. What's your major?"

"Films. I'm crazy about cameras, and I'd like to study directing. But also liberal arts."

"Me, too, I mean liberal arts. I expect to go to Berkeley."

"That right? Where are you from?"

"Carson Heights."

"Neighbors. Maybe I know this brother of yours. What's your name?"

"Brett Jayson."

He whistled. "Any relation to Tommy Jayson?"

"That's him."

"Well, he's only in my sister's class. I'm Jeffrey Wilson."

Brett said slowly, "This is, well, totally awesome, isn't it? Like ESP at work for me."

He shot her a curious look.

An attractive, ivied red-brick building had come into view, with its well-kept lawns and, behind it, an expansive playing field.

Brett said, "Would you pull over for a moment, Jeffrey?"

They dismounted before they got to the main entrance, and he waited for her to explain. It was hard for Brett to find an opening. At last, she said, "Tommy doesn't know I'm coming."

"Does it matter?"

"You may not understand this," she stammered, "but . . . Tommy and I have never met."

"What?"

"It's a long story. But could you suggest someplace, away from his class, where Tommy and I could meet, alone?"

Jeffrey stared at her thoughtfully. Then he said, "I think I know just the place. Tommy writes for his school paper. He's story and poetry editor."

Brett started, and swallowed hard. "Really."

"He can be in the editorial office"—he looked at his wristwatch—"in about an hour. After his class. I can have him there, if you like. Alone."

"You can do that?"

"I'll show you the place."

They biked in silence to a wing of the schoolhouse—a whitewashed, tree-shaded building. Indoors, it resembled a small newsroom, with desks, typewriters, a copier, shelves of newspapers and magazines, wastebaskets overflowing.

"You can wait for Tommy here."

"Won't some other people . . . ?"

"This is the kids' own domain. They're all in class at this hour."

"And Tommy?"

"I'll get word to him that someone . . . important . . . has to see him here at once."

"Would you leave out the 'important,' please?"

"All right. Should I change it to . . . 'very pretty'?"

They laughed.

Brett said, "Thank you, Jeffrey, for understanding."

"My pleasure," said Jeffrey. "But maybe, sometime, you'd like to tell me that . . . long story. Say, over a long milk shake?"

Brett said, "Yes, I think I would."

Tommy stood in the doorway. He was taller than she had imagined, sporty in his checked shirt, blue jeans, and sneakers, his round spectacles giving his freckled face a wise, old look.

They stared at each other, across the years. Brett said softly, "Hello, Tommy."

"Hi."

"I'm Brett."

"I know. I saw you once."

"You did?"

"In Gram's house. My mom had driven up just as you were biking off somewhere."

"Really?"

The boy blurted out, "I thought it was stupid! I mean, I wanted to get out of the car, but I was locked in. Automatic control."

"I'm glad you felt that way, Tommy."

"My mom would kill me if she knew we met." He spoke sadly, as though Charlotte was there, looking over his shoulder.

"Does she need to know, Tommy?" Brett started at her own words, hearing again the judge's question.

Tommy said, "I guess . . . no."

"Come and sit down, Tommy. Here. I want to share something with you."

They sat together rather formally, staring at each other with curiosity. Brett's thoughts were on Petey as she fumbled for the right words. "In a way, it's my fault for waiting so long. I'm older, seventeen, and you're nearly fourteen now. . . ?"

Tommy nodded.

"We're not infants. We have minds of our own. We have rights as . . . as sister and brother. Don't you agree, Tommy?"

"Yeah, but . . ."

"Today, I decided to . . . to go for it!"

"This meeting? Why?"

"Because, Tommy, I've just come back from a funeral in New York. One of my best friends. He couldn't take it anymore, the shoving around from place to place, the separation from his brother. . . ." Her voice was breaking. Tommy looked alarmed.

"Hey, don't cry," he said.

"I won't. I've done my crying. I want to tell you about him—Mac-the-Knife."

Tommy laughed, a spontaneous break from the tension: "Mac-the-Knife?"

She told him then about Second-Chance House and Mac and Petey and Brownie. She told him about her mama, who was ill; of how Gram and T.J. had sent for her, cared for her, and shielded and loved her since she was his, Tommy's age. She told him, watching his face twist in disbelief and sadness, how *their* father, Brett Sr., had literally thrown her away—denied her existence—after he married Tommy's mother, because of some sort of vow to each other; and she hadn't seen or heard from him since she was four.

"You need to know these things, Tommy. I don't want to hurt you. But they have to be said."

Tommy asked slowly, "Do you hate him?"

"I don't know. I used to. But I grew so thankful to be in Carson Heights with a family who cared about me that I stopped thinking about that. But, Tommy, I never stopped thinking about you."

The boy nodded, his eyes troubled with some private thoughts. "I have to get back now, Brett."

She walked him to the door.

"I'm graduating soon, Tommy. Valedictorian."

"That's great."

"Will you come?"

He wavered. "I'd have to tell them. . . ."

"Think about it. Meantime, want me to come again?"

Tommy adjusted his glasses and took a moment. "How would next week be, here, after classes?"

She grabbed him then, and hugged and kissed him. And he held her to him. Tight.

At dinner that evening, Brett told Gram and T.J. of her meeting with Tommy. They listened in silence, as she also told them what had triggered it: the counseling by the judge and Brownie.

T.J. leaned forward, looking worried. "You may have made life hard for Tommy at home, you know. Not to mention for us, uh, with Charlotte."

"No harder than it is already," Gram said briskly.

Brett said, "I had to, as the judge told me, go for it, T.J. If I'd told you beforehand, I might have been stopped. Well, by feeling guilty, not wanting to . . . interfere."

"Would we have stopped her?" he asked Gram.

"Maybe. I don't know," said Gram. "Now at last, thank God, we can stop this charade. You did right, Brett, to go for it."

17

It was a pathetic letter waiting for Brett later that week after school, scrawled and wavering on blue-ruled paper like a child's homework assignment:

Dearest Brett,
I'm writing from this goddamn prison,
where I landed this time instead of back in
Bellevue. They say I was into prostitution.
Lies. That bastard King wouldn't bail me out,
and the judge couldn't care less, so here I'm
stuck. When I get out, I won't go back to
King. But, baby, if only I could get the fare to
come to you in California. Your Brownie told
me to write you.

Brett, baby, I need *someone.* You're all I've
got. Could you get the money for me? Or the
airline ticket? I love you, always—but do it
soon, okay?

Mama

Whenever Brett had thought about Mama since leaving
Second-Chance House three years ago, it was with mixed
emotions of love and fear. During her brief stay in New
York for Mac's funeral, she had tried with Brownie to find
Mama. To no avail. Mama had moved from place to place.
Had she really been on the streets?

Brett showed the letter to her grandparents. The only
time they had met their daughter-in-law Joyce was just after
Brett was born: They had flown to New York to see their
first grandchild, and to give the almost penniless newlyweds
a large check to start them out. Now, they pondered the
letter and the problems it presented.

"I don't know, Brett," T.J. began anxiously. "You're
doing so well now—head of your class, getting ready for
college. And . . . and you've been happy here with us . . .?"

"Oh, T.J., the happiest I've been in my whole life!" Brett
burst out. "I think she's only desperate for some help."

"And that we can give her," said Gram firmly. "She
surely needs to get far away from all those people. She's
Brett's mother. . . ."

"Well, of course she is," T.J. said gruffly. "I'm just concerned how she'd fit into, well, small-town life."

"We'll never know till she tries, will we?" said Gram.
"We can stake her to a furnished place, maybe in those
rental apartments near the shopping mall. And, Brett, per-

haps you can persuade her to get counseling or psychiatric help."

"You're wonderful!" cried Brett. "I just know she'll get well here. Near to us."

"Near to us!" Gram repeated, her gentle face creasing into a wide smile. "What a funny thing it is, T.J.: For the first time, all our children and grandchildren will be near to us."

"And you know what else?" said T.J., getting into the spirit of it. "Sometimes kids are smarter than us adults."

"What do you mean?" asked Brett.

"Life's full of risks," said T.J. "The brave ones don't mind taking them on."

Brett kissed him. "Then you don't mind that I risked meeting Tommy?"

"I guess I don't. Because I'm thinking the day has to come when you'll meet with your father. And have a few questions for him?"

Brett said quietly, "Maybe. For Charlotte, too."

"It's time," said Gram.

T.J. mailed the airline ticket to Mama that day. He enclosed a note saying he'd be at the airport to drive her to Carson Heights, that they were looking forward to the reunion, that a good, new beginning could be worked out. Brett and Gram added loving and encouraging postscripts.

In the ornate arcade of Ye Flavor Factorie in the shopping mall, Brett and Jeffrey sat facing each other at a wrought-iron table, enjoying their orders of waffles spread with blueberries and whipped cream.

"They're awesome!" exclaimed Brett.

"Better than a milk shake?" Jeffrey teased, forking up a huge mouthful.

"Delicious. Or should I say deliciously fattening?"

They laughed like old friends, though they had known each other only a few weeks. Tacitly, they now followed a routine: Jeffrey would pick her up in Carson Heights in his old Ford, and drive her to the San Vision school's editorial offices for her visits with Tommy. Jeffrey would wait for her in the car, while Tommy showed her the coming new edition; and she'd show Tommy her poems or writings. She told Tommy also that her mother would be coming to Carson Heights. They always made plans for the next visit.

Now as she and Jeffrey sat relaxing, Brett felt more than ever drawn to the handsome, urbane young man who knew how to enter the feelings of others without asking questions. But now he did.

"I'm curious about that, uh, long story, Brett. Ready to clue me in?"

She looked at him with the old pain beginning to stab her stomach. "You want to hear the saga of my life?" she tried to joke.

"Not really," he said, gone serious. "Just some of the highlights. Like why you've got to meet Tommy in secret."

"Then I'd have to take you back a bit."

"Only if you want to, Brett."

"Yes. I want to."

They had finished their food—he had chosen the moment for his question carefully—and they sat contemplating each other. In some strange way, as she began, she felt the old, affectionate presence of Mac, her protector. She told him

126

about New York in the old days, happy days with Daddy. She stuck to the highlights, and told of some kids she'd known, after the divorce, in the foster homes and group homes and their deprivations—the throwaway generation to which she belonged. She saw Jeffrey draw back in disbelief. Only once did she stumble, when she described the drug scene and her beatings, and her life at Second-Chance House with Mac and Petey. Finally, she described the understanding judge who united her with her grandparents, and persuaded her to seek Tommy.

It was late when she finished, long shadows starting from the cathedral-style, glassed ceiling of the mall. He was a good listener, for which she was grateful.

"You're very solemn, Jeffrey," she said, her hand at her aching temple.

He took the hand in his. "I'm just glad that you shared this with me, Brett. Trusted me."

"And I'm glad we met on that road."

"I'll take you home now, Brett."

He linked her arm in his as they went to his car in the parking lot. He was very quiet on the drive to Carson Heights and her home. He said, "I guess most of us in small towns are pretty sheltered."

"Not really," said Brett. "Mac and Petey started out in a small town."

He nodded. "I'm learning. . . . Hey, you know what? My parents asked me if we're going together."

"Are we?"

He gave his great, infectious laugh. "We sure are! Well, aren't we?"

She smiled back at him, a little dazed. "We sure are," she said.

"Know what I mostly love about you, Brett? Those wise, unafraid blue eyes!"

He leaned forward and kissed her on her eyes and on her lips. Then held her close to him.

Mama was installed in a pleasant, studio-type apartment, a short bike ride from Brett's home. She looked embarrassed by her shabby appearance. Her once graceful figure was wasted, topped by badly dyed reddish hair, like a defiant slap at her misery.

She had held in her emotions as she thanked Gram and T.J. for "being so helpful . . . never forget your kindness." But after they left, she paced the small room in a sudden reversal of mood.

"That bastard in New York!" she burst out. "He didn't lift a finger to help me. I could have rotted in prison!"

"Mama, you have to stop this now."

"I'll make him pay!"

"No! Forget it! Forget him! There've been too many . . . bastards, Mama!"

"Oh, baby, you're so right. What am I saying?"

Brett stammered, "I mean, we're all hoping that you'll make a new start here, get some counseling."

Mama stopped pacing. She stared at Brett, her anger fading as she seemed to remember where she was. "Oh, Brett, forgive me. Can you ever forgive me? And yes, help me, baby. I'll be good, you'll see, I'll be very good. You're so grown-up. So beautiful."

She sat next to Brett on the studio couch, locking her hands together, looking prayerfully into her daughter's eyes. Subdued.

"I've been a rotten mother, haven't I?"

Brett kissed her. "Hush," she said. "I'll help you."

In that moment, holding the broken, fearful woman, feeling her mother's pain, she was remembering T.J.'s words: "Sometimes kids are smarter than us adults."

18

Charlotte Jayson was never happier in her whole life. She had found a secretarial job with a realty firm, which was perfect for a career, she told her husband. "I'll be learning the business at firsthand, until I study and qualify for my own real estate license. There's big money in selling real estate."

These days, she went about her tasks singing, well satisfied that her plans, stubbornly developed over the years, had worked to everyone's advantage. Brett was immersed in and apparently content with the computer systems he innovated and now directed, though the complex personnel training and supervision meant long hours, and often days away from home; the new systems took him to branches in other cities of California.

Charlotte bore the separations with unusual patience, since their combined salaries meant better, more gracious living for the family.

True, Tommy seemed rather withdrawn of late. She tried to draw him out, but he turned her questions off with shrugs or a polite denial, saying, "No problem." What she found unsettling was the lingering, sometimes reproachful look he would send her.

"What's wrong with you then?" she demanded at last, unable to contain her frustration.

"Nothing."

"I thought you were happy in this school. You've got friends, you're an editor on the paper, your father and I are pleased with your grades. So what's wrong? Tell me."

"You wouldn't like it if I told you."

"Wouldn't like what?" she asked angrily.

"I can handle it."

"What can you handle, Tommy?"

And he would shrug it off. Charlotte asked his father to take a hand. He got no further than Charlotte with his son.

There was no way, Tommy told himself defiantly, they were going to cut off his meetings with his sister. One day, they were bound to find out. But that day, he hoped, was in the far future.

He was wrong.

Charlotte's curiosity got the better of her. Unannounced, she paid a visit to Tommy's school. The social worker there was a neighbor, so her visit seemed routine, by a new parent.

Charlotte said with a smile, "Thought I'd catch up with my son's progress here."

"Oh, Tommy's fine—doing splendidly from all I hear."

"No problems?"

"None that have come to my attention. Why do you ask?"

"Well, that's what I'm here for—to ask," Charlotte said, masking her sharp reaction with the smile.

The social worker, nonplussed for a moment, said, "Well, we can have Tommy in while you're here, Mrs. Jayson."

"No, no. It's just that my husband and I are aware of some, uh, change in Tommy at home."

"What sort of change?"

"He's gone suddenly sort of introverted. You know, inward. Too quiet. As though he's got some"—she laughed uneasily—"huge problem weighing on him that he doesn't want us to know about."

The social worker said, "Ah, well, you realize that all teenagers have their, uh, private lives, private problems from time to time. Part of growing up. Tommy's rather new here, a very sensitive boy. . . ."

"But I know all that," said Charlotte restlessly. "Perhaps if I knew whom he sees in school, or after school. . . ."

"I can't help you there, unless I have Tommy in for a talk."

"Well, why don't I play it by ear today," Charlotte said with sudden decision. "Get a schedule of his classes, what time he goes to his editorial duties, so on?"

The worker looked dubious. But, she considered, Mrs. Jayson was a concerned parent. She picked up the telephone, dialed the registrar's office, and got the times of Tommy's classes. "I would suggest," she said, handing the list to Charlotte, "that you see the teachers after class, so as not to disrupt things."

"Naturally," said Charlotte. "Thank you."

In the late afternoon, as Charlotte made her way to the editorial offices, she pondered the teachers' reports with mixed emotions. All were positive and enthusiastic: Tommy was cooperative, studious, a good student who only "hated wasting time at gym." An old story, that. Was she then imagining things? Was she overreacting?

Two older boys were in the editorial offices as she entered, one at the files, the other at a desk, pecking away at a typewriter. A portable radio was playing some rock music.

She introduced herself, and they cordially invited her to sit at Tommy's desk while waiting for him. Standing between metal bookends on the desk were books of poetry, a dictionary, and a thesaurus. A double desk tray was full, apparently with contributions of stories and articles. On Tommy's large green blotter was a handful he had selected.

Sitting at her son's desk, touching some of the work before him, she felt renewed delight that Tommy, younger than the other boys, had been chosen for such specialized work. She did wonder how he would react when he saw her. She intended to tell him that she had been invited, that very day, because of her interest in the school, to be a candidate for the board of the Parent-Teachers Association, San Vision branch. He would certainly be proud of that.

In the busy room, while the radio turned to some hard rock, which always set her on edge, she picked idly at the selected papers before her. One in particular caught her eye: In contrast to the others, which were handwritten, this one was short and carefully typed. She drew it to her, and read:

I was hurting too much,
But that's in the past.
Can I make it now?
Will the new mood last?

There were unseen dangers,
Will I prefer those
To the new dangers here
That I must oppose?

Oh, when and where does
The healing process begin?
And who is to say
What was fair, what is sin?

It was signed, *Brett Jayson, 17, Carson Heights High School.*
Charlotte sat as though hypnotized. The color drained
from her face, and her body went rigid. All the pleasure of
the day evaporated as she stared at the signature. It was as
though the wall she had so painstakingly built around her
family had come crashing down around her. A powerful
urge seized her: to take the paper and shred it as she had
shredded a letter long ago. She was still staring at the paper
when Tommy bounced into the room. He stopped short as
he took in both mother and paper.

"Hi, Mom," he said tentatively.

Charlotte stood up. She was conscious of curious looks
from the other boys and the hard rock drumming on her
nerves. With great effort, she slung her tote bag over her

shoulder, waved good-bye to the two boys, and said, "We'll talk at home" as she brushed by the astonished Tommy and marched to her car.

"Our two schools sometimes exchange items for their papers," Tommy began to explain. "I thought by using this poem by Brett"—he saw his mother wince at the name—"it would be the best way to tell you we know each other. It was my idea."

Charlotte said harshly, "Your idea to do this shameful thing behind our backs!"

"What's shameful about knowing my sister?" Tommy asked, trying to stand his ground.

"She's not your sister! She's no one to us! Get that through your head, once and for all!"

Ever since Charlotte left the school, her anger had been mounting until she fantasized that her home, her family, her new life were all put at risk by "that girl." Now, as her husband sat silent and tight-lipped, witnessing the strange drama between mother and son, he tried to close his mind to the guilt that always stabbed him whenever he heard his daughter mentioned. Tommy had brought the poem home and shown it to his father. He was still holding it, staring at it, rereading it, when Charlotte shouted at him, "Why don't *you* say something to him? And stop *nursing* that goddamn thing."

He shook his head, unable to face his son's hard look. Unable to absorb his son's reply to Charlotte: "She's my sister. Besides," Tommy added bravely, "I like her."

"You're never to see her again, you hear!"

Tommy picked up his books, took the poem from his father, and headed for his room.

"Did you hear me, Tommy?"

"Yes."

"I want your promise. . . ."

"No, Mom."

"What? Did you hear that? He's defying me!"

Brett said wearily, "For God's sake, Charlotte, can't you drop it for now?"

She wheeled on her husband, her anger finding a new focus. Beside herself, she screamed, "I see it all! You'd like to destroy the . . . the conditions we agreed on, about never any of us seeing that girl or her mother. They don't exist! They never existed! Wasn't that our agreement?"

Tommy said, "How could you make such a promise? Brett exists. She has your name, Dad!"

"Stop right there, young man," Charlotte stormed. "Don't you talk to your father in that tone!"

Brett broke in suddenly, "No, he has a right to. It *was* a rotten condition from the first. I've sometimes thought, now that my daughter lives in the next town . . ."

Charlotte was rushing on, unheeding of the interruption, "And let me tell you this!" Her voice turned dangerous. "If ever you try to bring that girl here, I'll use my gun."

Brett sat straight up then. "Oh, come off it, Charlotte. Such threats are stupid."

"Call it what you like . . . but I would," said Charlotte.

"That's just terrible," said Tommy, "to say such a thing. Anyway, she'd never come here. I don't think she cares about you and Dad. Not anymore."

He went into his room and closed the door.

19

Charlotte wasted no time. Next day, she telephoned Gram "on urgent business" and arranged to go over that evening, "provided as usual that . . . Brett won't be there." She had difficulty getting the girl's name out.

Gram said, "I can't be sure about that tonight. She's in school, working on her graduation paper."

"Just see she's not there while we talk," Charlotte ordered harshly.

Gram hesitated. She could almost guess the reason for the urgent visit, now that the children were seeing each other. She said, trying for calm before the storm, "Well, all of you come for a potluck dinner, Charlotte. You know how T.J. loves to do a barbecue, and we can eat in the back garden—lots of privacy there."

"I don't want to put you to any trouble," Charlotte said, softening at the invitation.

"Not at all. Say about six-thirty? You can bring dessert, Charlotte—one of your delicious pies?"

Gram hung up slowly, feeling some despair. She hated scenes, but this moment had to come. Anyway, she told herself, best to have it and be done with it. After all the years of denial, the truth might at last have its way. It was with renewed shock she realized that in all the time Brett had lived with them, she and her father—their son—had never had a face-to-face meeting.

"Now let destiny take its course," she told herself. She even felt a tiny thrill of conspiracy.

The garden, in the early California evening, was inviting and cool, scented with the night jasmine and blossoming borders at the hedges. The sun was beginning to set in the still-blue sky, while the moon was already faintly showing up like a watch crystal.

"Pretty evening," said T.J. "Pretty table you've set, Gram."

He had donned his striped barbecue apron and was happily busy with the coals and spit for cooking spareribs, and preparing his specialty: a curry sauce to enhance the flavor, "while burning a hole in the stomach," Gram liked to tease.

The guests arrived bearing gifts: Charlotte with her pie; son Brett with a souvenir for his father's desk—a miniature computer paperweight; and grandson Tommy with a carbon copy of a cartoon he had sketched for the school paper; it was of a senior boy and girl in graduation gowns with tasseled mortarboards on their heads, and a word-balloon issuing from the boy's mouth saying, "Cheers! We're No. 1!"

Charlotte waited until the dessert before stating her urgent business. She was aware that her husband got up and left the table as soon as she began, and that Tommy looked after him desperately.

"You've got a troublemaker in this house," she plunged in. "She's been seeing Tommy, giving him . . . things, writing to him, all behind my back. Well, it has to stop. You must see that."

T.J. began in a puzzled tone, "What on earth . . .?"

Gram said, "Charlotte is referring to the children seeing each other. That right?"

"Now, isn't that nice?" said T.J., feigning surprise as he sliced the pie.

"No, it's not, and you know it's not!" Charlotte said, clasping her hands so tightly that the knuckles whitened. "I won't stand for this interference in my home, with my family."

"And what does Tommy have to say?" asked T.J., going grim as he placed a portion of pie on his grandson's plate.

Before Tommy could answer, Charlotte snapped, "We've discussed this whole matter, and I just wanted you to know what's going on. But I suddenly realize," she went on, getting shrill, "you've known all along."

Gram said, "Please understand one thing, Charlotte. Brett makes her own decisions. She's not an infant. In fact, she's very grown up and she and Tommy have so much in common—their interests, their writings, and . . ."

"You can stop right there," Charlotte said. She pushed her dessert away. "You've always known about our marriage agreement. That's the way we both wanted it. We were starting all over. You know that! And I won't have this . . . this street punk breaking into . . ."

"What did you call our granddaughter?" T.J. interrupted icily.

"Well, that's what she was," Charlotte rushed on, "like her mother before her, on the street, messing with drugs, landing in court. We know!"

Gram said with uncharacteristic anger, "If that's your urgent business, Charlotte, take it somewhere else. Brett is loved in this house. And just look at the effect you're having on Tommy!"

The boy was slumped in his seat, staring at his mother with something like disgust.

Charlotte said, "Tommy will understand when he's old enough."

A dreadful silence ensued, now clouding the garden party like a sinister shadow. In weird contrast, the birds in the oleanders were trilling their evensongs, skipping about in the high hedges, playing with one another. Then a screen door was heard banging indoors, and a cheery voice came from the family room, asking, "Anybody home?"

Brett stood before them, flushed and windblown from biking, her arms book-laden. The silent family turned as one to face her. For the first time in her life, Brett was seeing the family together.

In that moment, all she could think of was, "Hi, everyone."

140

T.J. broke the tension. "I've got some great spareribs and fries just waiting for you, Brett. . . ."

"Thanks, T.J., but Mama is expecting me. I only came home to tell you, and dump my books."

Without moving her head, Brett was conscious of the tall, graying, slightly stooped man walking toward the table, taking a stand behind Tommy, putting a hand on his shoulder. She remained transfixed. Was this the moment of truth then? Was this how confrontations happened? Was this the time of reckoning, of revenge?

She felt a rush of blood to her head as she stood, mutely, staring now at the man she had once so loved and yearned for, and had been denied. She pressed the books hard to her breast until they hurt her, as she looked at him—a stranger—who was silently staring back.

In the charged atmosphere, Gram, her lovely, lined face worried and sad, took a few steps toward Brett. But Brett was quite calm as she heard herself saying to the stranger, without any preamble, "I think you should know—I stopped hating you some time ago."

Then Charlotte shoved her chair back, saying abrasively, "Time for us to leave. Come on, you two."

But the man, not heeding Charlotte or anyone else, muttered, "If you managed to see Tommy, if you took that on yourself, why didn't you . . .?"

"After all these years?" cried Brett. "After you denied me all these years? You've known where I live. I wrote to you. I sent you my poems. You never answered. All right, even if you never got them for some reason . . ." She saw Tommy start. ". . . shouldn't you have tried somehow to find me, to care about what was happening to me? The truth is," she went on with measured contempt, "you never gave a shit about me!"

The man's hand gripped Tommy's shoulder as though he couldn't trust himself to move or speak. Then Charlotte was pulling Tommy from his grasp and stamping away from the table, shouting, "I said she was a punk and I'm right! Now, come on!"

T.J. said uneasily, "Why don't we all sit down together and just . . ."

Brett said, "It's all right, T.J. Don't be nervous. I just want *him* to know that I do have a father—you, T.J.! You and Gram—you've saved my life. So what I thought of as denial by him stopped bothering me."

Even Charlotte was listening for a moment, as though fascinated by the girl. "It did interest me once"—Brett was looking evenly at her father—"whether to confront you alone, and ask you flat out: Why do you listen to her? Where's your own mind?"

Charlotte said, beside herself, "I told you she was a troublemaker. Come on, you two! Thanks for the dinner."

Holding on to Tommy, she made for the back gate to avoid Brett.

"See you, Tommy," Brett called.

"No, you won't!" Charlotte yelled.

"'Bye, Brett," Tommy said.

Silently, his father followed them to their car. Gram and T.J. watched their departure in sorrowful silence.

Gram said, "Come and sit with us, child."

Brett ran to them, hugged them. She held back her emotions to spare them any more grief. After all, he was their

son, too; they must love him. She said, "Tommy and I—
we'll go on seeing each other, won't we?"

"Of course," T.J. said. He showed her Tommy's cartoon.
"As you see, with Tommy you're 'No. 1.' "

Gram said softly, "I don't know why your father—our
own clever son—is such a fool!"

"I lucked out," said Brett. "I *have* a father."

She kissed T.J., and it was his turn to flush. "What you
said to him, Brett—that was a class act. He's had it coming.
And Charlotte has a separate problem. She has an obsession,
child. Very sick," he said.

"Put it all behind you, Brett," said Gram.

"I'm okay. A bit shaky, maybe," said Brett with a small
laugh.

"Let me get you something to eat," Gram urged.

"One of my spareribs," said T.J. "Just take a minute to
heat this beauty up."

"Would you save it for me, T.J.?" said Brett. "I promised
Mama I'd see her. Do you mind? I'm afraid . . . I think
Mama's in some trouble."

Charlotte, at the wheel of the car, drove her family home
in brooding silence. Her husband sat in the backseat, as
though wanting to avoid her, or so she thought. She erupted
after he opened the front door.

"Of course, it was all your parents' doing!"

"What was?"

"Don't give me that! They stage-managed things so *she'd*
be there, with us!"

"Oh, nonsense," he said wearily. "She lives there. It's her
home." Even as he uttered the words, he was thinking it

was the only real, caring home she'd had for years. He felt the old stab of guilt.

Charlotte was rushing on, "And you also let that slut get away with her garbage about us!"

"Don't say stuff like that, Mom," Tommy muttered.

"You stay out of this!"

Brett stared at her moodily. And in that moment, Charlotte was shaken by such distaste in his look that she recoiled from it, turning away. There were times, especially since his transfer to the Coast and the reunion with his parents, when she felt torn and frustrated by his moods, which, she told herself, could threaten the treasured life she'd built for them. He had never questioned her good intentions before. Not until yesterday, when he had called their commitment rotten from the first. Did he no longer realize that everything she did in life was out of love for them, to shield him and Tommy from the wrong and bad outside influences?

Dimly, she became aware of Tommy's insistence: "Was it true, Dad—what my sister said?"

"Don't call her that, Tommy," said Charlotte.

"Was it?"

"Stop pestering your father."

But his father said, "I've been thinking, Tommy—that one of those times when you plan to meet *your sister*"—he emphasized the words—"you might take me along. Then perhaps I could try to explain. . . ."

Charlotte wheeled on them both, her voice gone dangerous again. "Forget it! I won't stand for it, you hear!"

Brett replied with the look that she had come to fear. "Yes," he said, "we hear."

20

Mama had never liked to cook, and now a cheese-and-tomato pizza from the supermarket where she clerked adorned the table. She got a carton of milk and a jar of instant coffee from the refrigerator. The begonia plant, brought by Brett on a previous visit, was the centerpiece.

Brett said, arranging dishes and napkins, making it sound casual, "I saw Daddy tonight. First time. He was at Gram's with Charlotte and Tommy when I came from school."

"So?"

"So nothing, Mama. Except it . . . did hurt."

"Naturally, baby, after all these years. Did he ask about me?" She sounded fretful.

Brett started. "Why, no. He didn't say much of anything. Charlotte rushed him and Tommy out."

"She would."

"T.J. says she has an obsession."

"That's for sure."

They ate in silence, Brett waiting for her mother to say what was wrong. She was worried about Mama's appearance and restlessness. Her makeup was heavy and careless, the rouged cheeks making her look clownish. They nibbled at the pizza, until Mama at last burst out, "I hate it at that damn checkout counter. Wears me down. All those people with checkbooks and credit cards, and screaming kids, and loading their groceries . . . and everything. I'm sick of it, Brett."

"So when you come home, you have a drink?"

"I didn't say that."

"You didn't have to."

"Baby, I've tried. You know I have tried!" She left the table. "I really hate drinking alone, but . . ."

"You promised. . . ."

Mama walked around, stumbling a little, forlorn. "I'm lonely here, Brett. I'm scared. I can't get used to this place. It's . . . well, I don't fit in."

"Just give yourself time, Mama. I had to."

"I don't know if I can hack it, Brett."

"We'll help you. I'll come more often. . . ."

"Darling, after summer, you'll be off to college somewhere, won't you?"

"Well, yes, but . . ."

"Anyway, I'm a drag on everyone. I know it."

"Mama, what is it? What's really wrong?"

She came over and kissed the top of Brett's head, and said uneasily, "Brett, baby, I heard from King."

"How could you," cried Brett, "unless you wrote him?"

"Well, he misses me. He was always saying he wanted to quit New York. All his friends are in jail or dead," said Mama, her hands fluttering. "He wrote back he's going to be in Los Angeles soon and . . . well, he expects me to join him in L.A."

"That horrible man! That pimp! You'd do that, Mama?"

"I can't hack it here, baby. It's too heavy."

Brett felt a nausea overtake her, and a surging anger at all that had happened that evening, at everyone, at Mama. "Go and wash your goddamned face! You look like a tramp!" she cried.

Mama's shoulders sagged. Then suddenly she lunged at Brett and slapped her face hard.

"Don't say that! Don't ever think that!"

Then she was hugging Brett to her, sobbing and smoothing the bruised cheek. "I'm sorry, baby, please, please forgive me!"

And Brett held her, murmuring out of her shock, "It's all right. It was my fault. It's been such a hateful day, Mama."

Neither of them went back to the table to eat. They sat on the couch, holding hands, as though, Brett thought desperately, it was like good-bye time again.

Mama walked her to her bike.

"You won't go to him, Mama, will you? Please don't go back to him."

"It's going to be all right, baby. Don't worry. Take care."

As Brett biked toward home, she was hardly aware of her surroundings—the leafy streets with their trim, storybook houses, manicured lawns, trim hedges. She felt far from the quiet, sensible scene, like the outsider of her poems, shattered by the traumas of the evening. She seemed to be biking into the haze of a broken old mirror. She could make out her father's image and Mama in the earlier, happier days in New York. Then the image broke again and faded to the men that Mama brought around, and the places she hid from them. It splintered more, and there was vaguely distorted Cathy and her wrenching bitterness about her stepfather's abuse; and old Mrs. Benton worrying about the kids in her care. She could see Michelle again, bullying and beating her half to death because of the drug pushers. The mirror images faded out altogether, except for the picture of Mac and Petey and Brownie, which she held on to, lovingly.

When the tears began to blind her, she got off the bike and walked it. Alone on the quiet streets, she realized that it was only in these last few weeks, since Mac's funeral, that she had been conjuring up more than once the old, bad years that she had thought she had put behind her. But events were conspiring to remind her—to force her to remember everything. Above all, to relive the rage that boiled up in kids who had been thrown away. She had been one of them, a full-fledged member of the throwaway generation. One of the thousands of kids who told themselves they must be bad, or why were they being punished, consigned forever to limbo?

It was clear. She could never forget. She wasn't expected to.

The house was silent, lights out in the garden, as though nothing unusual or cruel had taken place there. Brett wheeled her bike to the garage and went straight to her room. Gram and T.J. always retired early, and she undressed quickly and got into bed. Her head was pounding. She wanted the dark to enfold her, rub out the whole wretched evening, the heartache and memories, and give her a measure of peace.

The door opened a bit. Gram was asking softly, "You all right, darling?"

"I think so, Gram."

"I heard you come in. Waiting for you. So I kept some cocoa hot for us. I thought . . ."

"Oh, yes, Gram, please."

Gram set the tray with two cups of creamy cocoa on the bedside table. Then Brett was in her grandmother's arms, crying uncontrollably. Gram stroked her hair and waited. She wiped away Brett's tears and her own, and said in her best that's-enough voice, "We'll have our cocoa now, Brett."

"Oh, Gram, I love you. I feel safe. It's so wonderful to feel safe, Gram."

"Of course it is. Drink up, like a good girl."

Just before she fell asleep, Brett was aware that Gram, tactfully, had not asked about Mama.

21

Tommy himself took the initiative.

Later that week, he appeared at his grandparents' house after school to wait for Brett. "She has to copyread her poem which we're using."

"Will that make more trouble at home?"

"Maybe."

"You still want to publish it?"

"Not me alone," said Tommy. "Our editorial committee decides. Wanna read it?"

After she read the poem, Gram said, "How very strange. Brett anticipated what happened here the other evening, Tommy."

"That's what I thought, too. Funny, isn't it?"

Gram said, "With your help, Tommy, I think the healing process, as she calls it, can really begin."

Tommy nodded like a wise little man as he adjusted his glasses.

When Brett arrived with Jeffrey, they were not too surprised to find Tommy waiting for them. "They told us at school you'd be here. Why, Tommy?"

He blurted out, "Then it'll be my fault, if Mom finds out."

Brett wanted to hug him, but hesitated to embarrass him before the others, so instead she said, "I told you brains run in this family, Jeffrey."

Gram smiled as she left the young people to their meeting.

Jeffrey said, "Want to join us for waffles and blueberries, Tommy?"

"Oh, boy, sure! Brett can go over her poem there."

But Brett put in quickly, "Listen, Tommy, I don't think we should meet here in the future. It might become too, well, compromising for Gram."

"That's right—no more scenes." He shuddered.

"So I'd like to do something I've never done before," said Brett. "Show you both my secret place where I like to be alone, do my writing. Make it *our* secret place?"

The others looked eager. They got on their bikes, and she led the little convoy to the old cemetery at the edge of Carson Heights. In the late afternoon sunshine, she felt elated and, as always, at one with the beauty and serenity of the place.

If the others were astonished, they managed to conceal it, wondering where she was leading them. It was to the great, sheltering juniper tree, with its stout limb touching the ground as though awaiting her. She sank down on it, saying in reply to their questioning looks, "My private office. Here's where I write without interruption from living things."

Jeffrey stared around. "Well," he said solemnly, "it's a nice place to visit, but I wouldn't want to live here."

They laughed, and Tommy asked in wonder, "Hey, you come here alone? You're not afraid?"

Brett said, "It may seem weird to some people, but I never feel afraid or sad here; just glad to escape to my own secret place and thoughts."

"And now it's ours," exulted Tommy. He went off to explore.

"I don't think it's weird," said Jeffrey as he dropped beside her. "I think it's daring, even sort of romantic."

"Do you?"

"I do really." He drew her to him and kissed her long and tenderly. She had told him about the confrontation at her grandparents' house, and he felt more proud and protective of her than ever.

She read the poem, and shared it with Jeffrey, who was nodding his approval as Tommy came back from his foray. Tommy said, "Now for those waffles."

Brett laughed. "In a not-so-secret place."

There was a letter for Brett when she got home. Gram had propped it against a bookend in her room, and Brett recognized her mother's handwriting on the envelope. She stared at it for a long time. Even before she opened it, she felt she knew what the letter would say.

Dearest Brett,

I've tried writing this a dozen times and thrown them away, because how to tell you? Don't be too disgusted with me. I know how you've stood by me, baby, and I'll always love you for that. But, Brett, you saw it coming the other night. I can't hack it here anymore. I need the city and friends and the clubs. And whatever you think of King, he takes care of me, except this last time, and for that I intend to give him hell.

Yes, I'm going to him in L.A. He phoned and said he'd drive here and get me, but I knew you wouldn't want that. He's not so bad, and I need *someone,* Brett. I wish I could be here for graduation; but maybe it's better this way—leaving at this time so you don't have me to worry about. I'll let you know how I'm doing. After all, L.A. isn't the end of the earth.

Give my best wishes to everyone. Be strong and be happy, Brett.

> With love,
> Mama

Mama, how could you?

How could you trash everything and everyone?

How could you hurt Gram and T.J. this way?

And me—what about me? I had such hopes again, for you and me, Mama.

Don't you know that man will only trash you, Mama? Poor Mama. . . .

She showed the letter to Gram, who read it in silence.

"What she's really telling me," said Brett in a bitter tone, "is that she wants the booze and the drugs and, yes, the street . . . and he's her source. He'll make her pay, of course."

"Oh, Brett, how sad."

"She'll go down to the gutter again."

Gram said, "At least we tried. But there comes a time when people have to take responsibility for their actions."

Brett cried helplessly, "She's my mama, and I don't know what to do anymore."

"It's a relapsing illness she has, Brett."

"You don't think I should go after her? Bring her back?"

"It wouldn't do any good, dear. Not until she signals us again for help."

"Would you, Gram—I mean, help again?"

"I'm sure we would," said Gram. "T.J. and me—we believe in giving people a second chance. Even," she added with a wry smile, "the Charlottes of this world."

22

"That valedictory speech I wrote before I went to New York," Brett began as soon as she was alone with Miss Fleming, her social studies teacher. It was the last day of school, and students had left the classroom early. The room already looked strangely bereft.

"Yes, Brett?"

"I tore it up. It doesn't fit anymore."

"Doesn't fit?"

"My mood," said Brett.

"Well, as you know, the staff doesn't pass on what our honor students want to say. You're on your own."

"I appreciate that. But I've been drafting a totally new kind of speech, and, uh, I hoped you'd read it anyway."

Miss Fleming, tall and elegant in her silky navy blue pants

suit, studied her favorite pupil with a touch of concern. "Something in it bothering you?"

"Miss Fleming, I think it may come off like . . . an attack."

"Really? On whom?"

"Parents."

Fleming started. "Well, to use a current cliché, that's totally awesome. Whose parents?"

"It takes on people who have control of kids, or who reject them, throw them away."

"I see. Well, you realize the class president usually sticks to projections of the graduates' hopes and dreams, with at least," she added, "a smidgen of gratitude to parents, to the school."

"Oh, I love this school and my friends here," Brett burst out. "That won't be a smidgen. It's just that you above all know the kind of life I had before I came to live here. My grandparents—they saved my life. I could have gone like Mac-the-Knife. I was nearly destroyed."

"Therefore?"

"And therefore, I feel I have to be a witness—a witness who has to get the story out to people who don't know or haven't cared what's happening to the unwanted kids."

"You really think this is the time to do it, Brett? With all those happy graduates and their delighted parents sitting in the sunshine, wanting only to be flattered and told nice things?"

Fleming's tone was a touch cynical, but also worried. She sat on her desk, studying the earnest, flushed face of the other. Part of Brett's charm had always been her cool bearing and maturity, far beyond her seventeen years, which masked, however, a deep need for acceptance. She would probably give the speech with or without approval, Fleming reasoned, but at the moment, the girl wanted her reaction, her involvement.

"Have you a copy of the speech, Brett?"

Brett got it out of her schoolbag.

She went to a window and tried to focus on the green playing field where games of volleyball and baseball filled the air with the players' shouts and laughter. What if Fleming didn't support her? What if this teacher, whose sensitivity and friendship had helped her over the rough times, especially in this final year of emotional traumas, was opposed to such drama at graduation time? What if it looked as though she was taking revenge?

Fleming joined her at the window. "It's certainly different, and it should hold them."

"Oh, you think . . . How can I ever thank you?"

"By not leaving out a single thought in it," the teacher said in a measured tone, "and let the chips fall where they may."

The weekend before graduation was among the best times of Brett's life.

Jeffrey's parents had invited her to relax, forget school and tensions by spending that weekend aboard their houseboat, the *Dolphin*. It was anchored on a man-made lake some forty miles from Carson Heights, an old thirty-footer that was their retreat.

In glorious weather, she and Jeffrey and his sister Lucy went swimming and fishing off the boat, read a little, and mostly lazed the days away. Mr. Wilson, a strapping, white-haired man in his sixties, was a rod-and-reel magician. He caught the fish—three striped bass and a medium bluefish. And Jeffrey helped to haul them in with a long-handled net, groaning meanwhile that he couldn't even land a minnow.

Mrs. Wilson, dainty and gray-haired, her eyes snapping with laughter at her husband's feats, was sketching the scene. She was adept at painting seascapes on vases and plates, which she exhibited and sold at the China Boutique in the mall.

After fishing, they would stretch out and doze in the sunshine, Lucy bestirring herself from time to time to skip bread crusts on the water to the ducks swimming near the boat. Brett watched lazily, enchanted.

They dined on the catch, which Mrs. Wilson grilled on a portable stove in the galley, served up with buttered potatoes and green salad. Afterward, Mr. Wilson revved the motor and piloted the houseboat back to its slip, anchoring alongside the sail- and powerboats, like great birds nesting until morning.

At night, the young people used their sleeping bags on deck under the stars, while their elders slept below in the bunks. Lucy was first to fall asleep, "exhausted," she explained, "from fighting off all those sharks."

"It's been such fun," Brett murmured gratefully.

Gram was calling her. "You ready, Brett?"

"Ready for what, Gram?" Brett cried as she ran to the family room.

"Oh, didn't I tell you?" asked Gram in mock surprise. "We're going shopping."

"Are we now? What for?"

"T.J. said to come back with the sexiest dress, the prettiest shoes and stockings and purse in Carson Heights. He said, 'Shoot the works for our girl.' "

Brett giggled. "I'll bet he didn't say sexiest."

Gram held up a hand in protest. "I swear it."

"And just as I was planning to shock everyone with my old blue jeans and T.J.'s work shirt," said Brett slyly.

"Oh, you! Anyway, you may, as Fleming told you, shock them enough with your speech," said Gram.

Brett had offered to let her grandparents read her speech, but they had said no—"Surprise us."

Brett said, gone solemn, "I'm hoping it will stimulate, too—some of them."

23

Graduation Day began with a typical inland fog that hovered over Carson Heights for hours, threatening rain. But by noon, in true California style, the sky cleared and sunshine broke over the playing field, transformed by volunteers. It now resembled a lovely dell.

At the far end, a flag-bedecked speakers' platform held great tubs of flowers, and from each side of it, triple rows of seats for the graduates faced the prospective audience. The field itself, newly mowed, was hung with myriad colored lights that were looped over treetops and flagpoles, turning the scene into Christmas in June. The public section was alive with colorful paper streamers and balloons; and edging the field, beach umbrellas shaded tables in readiness for refreshments.

By four o'clock, with every seat taken, the school band struck up "America the Beautiful." A dozen cheerleaders went into their act, dazzling the audience with their pomponned gymnastics. Then the graduates, in long white dresses or white shirts and black trousers, filed in, to loud applause and whistles, some of the less inhibited calling out to a son or daughter in the parade. The warmly happy scene reflected sheer delight, as of one great, integrated family.

On the speakers' platform, Brett took her seat with the other honor students, the principal, and counselors. Looking radiant in her fitted white cotton dress with satin appliqué and cummerbund, she scanned the audience for Gram and T.J., finding them with Jeffrey in the second row. And next to them, Tommy.

"Oh, you Tommy," she thought, "you're going to catch it when you get home. Brave Tommy!"

The preliminaries didn't take long. The principal welcomed guests and graduates with a brief address, and the choir sang the school song. Then the band swung into a popular medley of "Home on the Range," "The Best Things in Life Are Free," and "God Bless America," the student conductor turning to the audience on the last number, urging them to sing along, which they cheerfully did.

When the applause died down, Miss Fleming, a stunning figure in a pink tailored suit and black lace jabot, stepped to the lectern. She called off the honors winners, each of whom went forward to receive the Founders Day Award to cheers. Brett was last to be called, and she remained at the lectern, as class president, to deliver her speech.

As she faced the immense, friendly throng, waiting in happy anticipation of her message, she felt the words drying up in her throat. An old dread began to knot her stomach, and her hands shook. The pages of her speech on the stand fluttered, and as she steadied them, she thought desperately: Would she only be talking to the wind? Wouldn't it be easier, wiser, to say a few bland things, add something from her old essay, and let it go at that?

Then Fleming was beside her, as though sensing her desperation, seeming to help her with the fluttering pages. Brett felt Fleming's hand on hers, heard her say with quiet affection, "Go, Brett."

She found her voice. It helped to be able to visualize among the audience those she'd once lived with, been thrown in with, loved, and hated; the judge would surely be "listening" to what she said here, and Mac and Petey and Brownie and, yes, Mama, too.

She got off quite firmly her preliminary remarks—in any case, she really meant them: her thanks to her grandparents, her teachers who had helped "this rank newcomer of only three years in Carson Heights," her gratitude for the great honor of representing her fellow students.

"And with all that support, what am I capable of today?" She plunged on. "Yes, I represent my fellow students, but I also represent the lost generation of kids. I have to tell you this, because I was one of the lost, shunted for most of my life from foster home to foster home. Until my grandparents here cared for me and loved me, and I learned because of them to trust adults again. But I was one of the fortunate ones. I happened to luck out.

"There are thousands of kids out there—maybe some here among you—who need to get lucky. Who need better than foster homes and group homes and juvenile jails and being treated like criminals or pieces of paper on a judge's desk, to be rubber-stamped and thrown away. But are we names and dates on pieces of paper? We're human beings, kids with rights and with feelings.

"I'm talking about the throwaway generation. I'm talking about kids who've known nothing but rejection—denial—in their lives: by natural parents or foster parents, by certain judges, by city and state systems. These are not just big-city kids. You find them in the small towns of America, too. Many of them become drifters—running from a system or from parents, denied love and stable homes. Is it any wonder that so many turn to drugs and alcohol and crime, and some to prostitution, to get shelter or money to eat?

"There are a million kids of this throwaway generation out there, right now, being passed from foster home to foster home; and passed over for adoption when they get what's called 'aging out'—too old to adopt at age twelve or thirteen or fourteen. Yes, there are good foster homes, or *all* the million kids would be on the street, shunted from one place to another.

"The system is crazy. It betrays not only kids who could be adopted, but also thousands of good people who want kids but can't afford to take them in and adopt."

She could feel the dreadful silence around her. Someone not far off was coughing fitfully. A child was crying and was hushed. Brett went on in a ringing voice, "I blame those who, in the words of one good judge, abdicate their responsibility to the kids. And I blame the system that's leaving too many kids, especially adolescent kids, in limbo. They have nowhere to turn for help. My friend Mac, who was my age, my protector in my last foster home, shot and killed himself because the brother he loved was taken from him and adopted, but no one wanted Mac."

Brett heard the audible gasp from the audience. She took a long moment before she managed to steady her voice, to cry passionately, "The kids I've been talking about need parents. Loving and devoted parents. And if that's denied them, then loving care from other family members or foster parents—decent people who can help them to feel like proud citizens of this country!

"Thank you very much."

As Brett took up her papers, there was an immense silence. Then from below the speakers' platform she heard applause begin. Thinly, at first, then it rose like a gathering chorus of applause and whistles. With a start, Brett realized it was coming from the kids themselves—her fellow graduates.

She felt the tears in her throat fill her eyes, which brimmed over as she stood there taking their cheers. They understood. And now, mixing with the kids' support, the applause from the audience itself. Fleming came to her, her own eyes quite misty, as she whispered, "Good girl."

She led Brett back to her seat. The band struck up with "Hail, Hail, the Gang's All Here." Then the principal was back at the lectern, calling each graduate's name, and handing out the diplomas.

"So, Miss Fleming, I got it off my chest," said Brett after the ceremony. "But will it do any good? Who was really listening? Was I only 'talking to the wind'?"

"Oh, you'd be surprised who was listening," Fleming said a bit airily. "I decided to get in touch with a friend of mine on the *Los Angeles Times,* told him he'd find a good story here at graduation. He came, Brett. He was listening, you can be sure. Or he doesn't have a date with me tonight!"

They were waiting for her at the refreshment tables, Gram and T.J. and Tommy and Jeffrey.

And standing alone near an exit sign, another figure, a tall, slightly stooped man, awkward-looking in his isolation. He was staring around and, as he caught sight of her, uncertain whether to come out of the shadows.

Brett had seen him stop at the edge of the happy crowd. Was he waiting for her to make the next move?

She didn't hesitate.

She turned sharply, and ran into the arms of Gram and T.J. and held them close.

Without moving her head, and not without a touch of sadness, Brett was aware that the tall, stooping figure had watched them. Then he was turning away, walking to the exit.

The joyful noises of parents and friends, delighting in their kids, followed him on his way out, as he went back into the shadows.

Gram was murmuring, "We're so proud of you, Brett."

T.J. could only stroke her hair, as though he was too bursting with pride to find words. The others looked on, beaming.

With one arm around Tommy and her other linked in Jeffrey's, Brett said, "There were so many years, so many times, when I felt lost and hated my life. Now," she said as the tears started slowly, "I know I like myself. I really do."

About the Author

GERTRUDE SAMUELS is an award-winning author and playwright, and former *New York Times* journalist. Among her works are *Run, Shelley, Run!*—judged a Best of the Best for Young Adults by the American Library Association—and *Adam's Daughter.*

Of this documentary novel, she states, "As a journalist and novelist, I have long been drawn to the plight of kids in trouble with the law and who are rejected by their parents or society. Basically, these children are desperate for stability in their lives, for someone who will be there for them and love them."

Ms. Samuels lives in New York City.